A Cause For All

Norman Finn

A CAUSE FOR ALL
Copyright © 2024 **Norman Finn**

ISBN (Paperback): 979-8-88764-467-7
ISBN (Hardback): 979-8-88764-469-1
ISBN (eBook): 979-8-88764-468-4

All rights reserved. No part of this book may be used or reproduced by any means, graphic, electronic, or mechanical, including photocopying, recording, taping or by information storage and retrieval system without the written permission of the author except in the case of brief quotations embodied in critical articles and reviews.

Because of the dynamic nature of the Internet, any web addresses or links contained in this book may have changed since publication and may no longer be valid. The views expressed in the work are solely those of the author and do not necessarily reflect the views of the publisher, and the publisher hereby disclaims any responsibility for them.

Printed in the United States of America.

Page88 LLC
447 Broadway, Suite 2028,
New York, New York 10013
www.page88books.com
1.201.537.3680

Dedication

To: Judith, Ted, Leslie, Taylor and Rachel Finn

"A man does what he must—in spite of personal consequences, in spite of obstacles and dangers and pressures—and that is the basis of all human morality."

—Winston Churchill

Acknowledgements

I SPENT CONSIDERABLE time researching the book as I did with *"I Shall Know Who I Am"*. Many of the references which were used came from the combined research for both manuscripts. The actual historical timeframe for both books ran continuously.

Like so many others, I became totally captivated by the history of the events and spent countless hours reading about this period as it relates to world history, not just the Middle East.

Historically, the book is quite accurate. The characters are fictional, except for Nasser, with whom I took the liberty of putting words into his mouth.

I reviewed my notes and photos of the two trips that I made to Egypt. Some of the key cities and destinations Michael visited were places that I had the opportunity to see. Those experiences were invaluable in developing the story. Being there was a great asset.

I owe a debt of gratitude to Marge Keohane for her ability to translate my handwritten pages into readable text. Dr. Ruth Khowais edited the manuscript and gave me comments and suggestions that enhanced the story.

Michael may return with some additional adventures. Let's see what the world will bring to his doorstep.

Chapter 1

ISRAEL WAS SAFE for the time being. Aron Harel and Joshua Zamir, Mossad agents, were trying to analyze past events in their proper perspective. It would be weeks, no...months, to truly understand the ramifications of the Egyptian operation. So much had transpired at the same time which initiated a whole new set of concerns which would eventually have to be addressed. They would have to weigh all the material to understand where they were in this continuing struggle to protect Israel.

In the meantime, they felt relieved for they had temporarily answered a volatile situation. They had destroyed the ability of ex-Nazis to develop V2 Rockets in Egypt. Israel had dealt a major blow to Nasser's programs and plots to wreak havoc on them. His Pan-Nationalism, the development of the United Arab Republic, Egypt, Syria and Iraq, was derailed and never able to get on track. None of this would have happened without enlisting the aid of Michael Janssen, an American who became a major factor in the success of the mission.

Michael had done more than his part in the ingenious plan to bring the Egyptian V2 program to ruin. He had been enlisted by the Mossad and gone to Egypt as an Arab-speaking entrepreneur. His business, fashion and manufacturing, paved the way for him to penetrate an international arms dealer's organization and Nasser's facilities. With the help of Egyptian nationals and the Mossad, Michael was able to bring the entire rocket program to destruction.

The analysis by Tel Aviv showed that, although they had been successful, the embers of conflict were still burning. The Arab coalition's desire for the destruction of Israel was not diminished. How it would re-appear was the question.

Michael was essentially exhausted. The ordeal had taken every ounce of strength to not only succeed, but to stay alive. As he looked back over the events of the past six months, it was hard to believe he had survived, not only physically, but mentally.

Michael wanted to get back to his life and his loves…the fashion business and Doria, his wife. He had accomplished a number of positive elements from this experience.

#1 As a Jew, he had done his part in protecting Israel.

#2 In his mind, his actions avenged his father's death at the hands of the Nazis. His father was killed because he was a Jew and spoke out against them.

#3 Under the most unusual circumstances, he had found the love of his life, Doria Sadat, an Egyptian. She played a primary role in working with Michael and Tel Aviv to help destroy the Nasser rocket program.

In spite of the success of the operation, Michael lay awake most nights, reliving the events. The experiences did not offer him closure.

His friend and fellow spy, Benjamin 'Bengy' Barak, had saved his life with a shot to the head of Hassan Streiger, the German/Egyptian arms dealer. Hassan had developed the rockets in Germany and planned to have Nasser launch them at Israel.

Michael could not forget Mr. Nsar's help in their escape. He had a major position in the Egyptian Secret Service, spying for Israel. Without his efforts, Michael and company would not have escaped.

There was Doria, director of Hassan's international cotton business and right-hand in all administrative matters. She was so in love with him and had paid the ultimate price as a traitor to her country. By becoming an Israeli spy, she had severed all ties with Egypt and burned the bridge by working with Michael. Doria's courage and cooperation were the deciding factors in the plans to destroy

- A Cause For All -

the threats to Israel. She did not believe in Nasser's plans for Pan-Nationalism, his expulsion of foreigners and Jews, nor his authoritarian regime.

Michael was now home in Boston with his family and was ecstatic to have his mother, Hannah, and sister, Rachel, around him. Hannah and his father met in Egypt. She came from a Sephardic Jewish family, fell in love with David, a non-Jew, and eloped, moving to Chicago. David Janssen became a Jew while working in Munich as a senior executive of Kruger International. In 1936, he was murdered by the 'Brown Shirts' when Michael was just six weeks old.

Michael yearned for his life to return to normalcy. There were Abe and Sarah Stone, brilliant retailers, but childless. Michael considered them his adopted parents. They had seen his fashion talent grow from an early age and gave him the resources to progress in their business. He had taken advantage of every opportunity for Michael was now heir apparent to their worldwide apparel firm. There wasn't any question that he had earned the right as he had the talent, ambition, and desire. Michael was now ready to assume leadership as the creative director and CEO of the firm. All the pieces were falling into place.

The first item on his agenda was marrying Doria. She needed to adjust to her new life, country and family. Doria had lived her life working in Egypt. Her only knowledge of the States were the stories that her father had told during his visits as an educator and lecturer. What made the transition easier was her sophistication and intellect. But, she was alone and there was only Michael. Her family was in Egypt and her beloved father had passed away, leaving only her mother in Alexandria.

Michael was well aware of the pressures and adjustments Doria had to face. Hannah and his sister, Rachel, took her under their wings and made it their priority to help her assimilate. Abe and Sarah adopted her as their 'additional child'. She fell into the same classification as Michael. They now had a daughter, as well as a son.

The wedding was more than they expected. Abe and Sarah had taken over as Doria's parents. "I have only one daughter and we shall give her a wedding we all shall remember." Abe invited all the key personnel of the company and Michael's friends. Aron, Joshua, and Bengy were sent tickets to attend. Michael and Doria were married by a Reform Rabbi, just as Michael's mother and father had been.

Doria was a spectacular bride in every way. She was statuesque, with a radiance about her that was beyond her natural beauty. So was the groom, standing over six feet tall with piercing dark eyes and perpetually bronzed skin, waiting for Doria to walk down the aisle. Rachel was the maid of honor and Bengy was the best man as Abe gave the bride away. It was a picture-perfect wedding and Hannah was beyond joy. She cried, wishing her David was there.

Chapter 2

LIFE WAS RETURNING to normal or, should we say, the new normal. Michael resumed his position with the company and started to re-learn what had transpired while he was gone.

He took Abe by the arm. "You have done a masterful job, not only with the financial numbers, but developing the right culture."

Abe was pleased. "I only followed your original plan and just kept adjusting as it was needed. Sarah did a great job building additions to the line."

"'I've had a few weeks to analyze where we are. We are at a critical point in our business. Do we push the envelope and expand at a greater rate than our original plan? Our profitability per store is way above our original projections. It seems everything is breaking our way. Do we gear up our earlier plan and push forward?"

"Michael, I think there is a middle ground. I am inclined to take this route until you have your feet firmly planted on the ground. You have been away from the business almost eight months. You need to become re-involved in every area." Michael was nodding in agreement. "I believe you are right. Let's visit this topic in a few months."

His forte was design, along with all the elements of product development. He was gifted, not only with an innate sense of merchandising and knowing what would sell, but he could create. His work in Egypt setting up a production line served the purpose of on-the-job training, giving him a great learning experience.

His game plan was to dress the customer from head to foot. It was not just "one-stop shopping" that he wanted to achieve. Michael wanted to create a look, almost a "uniform" for his following. He spent significant time developing footwear, as well as handbags, lining up resources that would build specific product to fit their model's image and specifications. Under Michael's leadership, his design team created these "looks" which presented a total fashion picture.

Doria was bonding with Hannah and Rachel. There was more than just a mutual respect for one another. Hannah's mission in life was to make Doria as comfortable as possible in her new surroundings. They both had Egyptian roots which bonded them together and made the transition easier.

Doria desired to convert to Judaism and Hannah brought her to Temple Israel to take part in conversion courses. Michael went along to talk with the Rabbi. He got the message that he should attend the conversion classes with Doria. The process brought them closer together. They were now becoming a complete family.

The couple purchased a condominium in Chestnut Hill, Massachusetts. It was Doria's decision to live in an apartment rather than a house. They felt the adjustment would be easier and it was important they spend time with one another. Their entire courtship was under the most unusual of circumstances, surrounded by danger, intrigue, and fear of being discovered.

The fashion business was demanding and Michael's day was ten hours or longer. They would escape every weekend, he showing her Cape Cod and the coast of Maine. She loved Vermont and wanted someday to have a vacation home in the mountains.

They fell in love under the strangest circumstances. Their romance was filled with every emotional issue you could possibly fathom. Fear, anxiety, and extreme stress were elements they faced daily. The knowledge that death and personal injury were everyday risks was always present. Both Michael and Doria had other people's lives in their hands. They needed time to heal for both had been away from the world while the operation in Egypt was being played out. They now were about to enter normal life.

But life was not so normal. The world was still threatened by the rumblings of conflict. It was difficult to shut your eyes and ears to what was transpiring around them.

The year 1965 was a year of dramatic change.

Lyndon Baines Johnson proclaimed the Great Society and was inaugurated as President.

Winston Churchill's funeral drew the largest assembly of statesmen in the world.

The Vietnam war heated up with operation "Rolling Stone Thunder's" aerial bombardment.

Bloody Sunday occurred with two hundred State Troopers attacking marchers in a Civil Rights March from Selma, Alabama to the state capital in Montgomery.

The first American troops arrived in Da Nang, Vietnam.

Lyndon Johnson made his "We Shall Overcome" speech and eventually put into law the Voting Rights Act of 1965.

Martin Luther King and twenty-five thousand civil rights marchers walked from Selma to Montgomery, Alabama.

Students at Berkeley College burned their draft cards.

The Beatles arrived in the USA.

West Germany and Israel established diplomatic relations.

In May, there was the largest anti-war march. President Johnson increased the troops in Vietnam from seventy-five thousand to one hundred twenty-five thousand.

LBJ signed the War on Poverty Bill which put the Social Security Act into law, establishing Medicare and Medicaid.

In Frankfurt, the Auschwitz trials convicted sixty-six personnel to life sentences.

LBJ signed the Immigration and Nationality Act of 1965 which ended quotas based on natural origin.

Thousands of Vietnam protesters picketed the White House and marched to the Washington Monument.

Charles DeGaulle was elected as French President.

At this time, the U.S. was deeply concerned about the movement of the Arab Bloc into Nasser's control and Soviet dominance. It hinged on the U.S. handling of supplying arms to Jordan. It was a challenging situation, balancing its priorities between Jordan and Israel. The U.S. felt a strong working Arab alliance with the Soviets was a direct threat to the entire region and Israel's security. The U.S. was ready to deliver tanks to Israel if the West Germans did not honor their commitment. They were obligated to deliver aircraft if the situation demanded it. LBJ was prepared to make extremely difficult decisions to support Israel's security.

This was the course of events that had set the stage. It demanded sacrifice fighting for a cause…a cause for all.

American policy toward the Middle East stemmed from the following:

1. The containment of Soviet and Chinese expansion in these areas.
2. To eliminate a super-power confrontation over the escalation of conflicts in this region.
3. To keep the flow of oil coming from the region through the Suez Canal.
4. A commitment to Israel's existence, primarily from the six million American Jews.

In 1965, there was a crisis surrounding the diplomatic relations between the Federal Republic of Germany and the governments of Israel and Egypt. The crisis was provoked by arms shipment from West Germany to Israel. This resulted in a setback for Nasser and gains for Israel as West Germany established diplomatic relations with Israel.

The weekends were just what they needed. Fall in New England was one of the wonders of the earth. Doria just couldn't believe the color, its intensity and brilliance. She was amazed by the warmth of the days and cool nights. She had found contentment with Michael for he was the perfect lover and friend, wanting to better her life in every way.

"Michael, I am extremely happy with our lives. I can't believe how lucky I am to be here in America with you." "Doria, I am the lucky one to be your husband." Doria hugged him.

"We have to talk about me and my life with you and what I would like to do. You have to remember that I was an administrator and responsible for an international business, dealing with clients from around the world. I cannot just clean the apartment."

Michael smiled. "Actually, I was waiting for you to say something. You are absolutely right. It would be a waste not to put you to work so I can live the lifestyle I always wanted." They laughed.

"I always envisioned us working together. Your skills are made for our business. You could be a major asset organizing and running everyday operations. Abe needs the help and, as the business has grown, it's more than one person can handle. You think I fell in love with you because of your body and good looks? You are mistaken. I need you to go to work so that in my old age, I can retire early!" Doria jumped into his arms, holding him close…"you are wonderful, my love."

"By the way, speak English. We are back in America!"

Michael sat down with Abe and laid out his plans for Doria and how they should bring her into the business. Abe was in total agreement. "We need her and I like the idea of family in key positions. Trust is always an issue and with Doria controlling the administration, we will always sleep soundly." Both Sarah and I will spend time with her. She needs to be exposed to all phases of the operation. We will make sure all our staff is aware of her entrance."

Michael did one step better. He brought all the key executives together at a lunch meeting with Abe, Sarah, and Doria. "I want to be very clear. Doria is about to enter this business. I would not bring her into this organization if I felt she did not have the ability to be an asset to the company. She ran a significant organization in Egypt that not only manufactured but wholesaled its product throughout the world. Her skills dealing on an international basis were an essential part of the position. This business is only for people who perform. If she does not, she is out. Let's welcome her to the fold."

Chapter 3

WALTER SCHMIDT THOUGHT he was fortunate to have escaped the destruction of Hassan Streiger's facilities in Essen. The Mossad had detonated the factory and the underground facility that had developed the V2 rockets that were sent to Egypt. By a stroke of luck, he had left the factory minutes before the blast and was actually considered dead in the aftermath of numerous unidentified bodies.

Schmidt had been the right-hand man to Hassan Streiger, the Egyptian/German arms dealer. He had a small interest in Hassan's operation and was a loyal follower of the Third Reich. He still had connections to the Odessa and those that escaped to South America and the Middle East.

Schmidt wanted revenge for he had lost friends in the blast and wanted to somehow kill the Jews who had destroyed his world and his dear friend, Hassan Streiger. Schmidt had connections to a far-right nationalism group in Germany that had been an off-shoot of the Odessa, developing escape plans for Nazis escaping the allies.

He was willing to finance a plan to kill the Jews and had been to Egypt on missions for Hassan and knew Doria long before Michael was involved. Hassan had confided in him and was part of the whole story of Fantastique. The Mossad used this British company, Fantastique, to develop the cover.... Schmidt was second in command. He was willing to do anything to bring the Jews down.

After the crushing defeat of Hassan and the V2 program, not much was known about where Michael and company had gone. The Israelis had done a masterful job cleaning up the shoot-out in Florence, leaving no clues.

Hassan and his henchmen were either dead or defeated.

Schmidt sent out a message through his contacts with the Odessa that he wanted to know the whereabouts of Michael and Doria. At the same time, he was more than concerned for his own life. Did the Israelis know that he was still alive? Did they know of his relationship with Hassan? He was determined to seek revenge and, at the same time, realized he was vulnerable.

Chapter 4

DORIA TOOK TO her new career immediately. Her skills acquired in Egypt shortened the learning curve and everyone was impressed. Her organizational skills were extraordinary, bringing the company into a new phase of efficiency. Both Abe and Sarah were impressed with her ability and know-how. In a matter of months, the administration end of the business was under her control and functioning extremely well.

Michael was developing all aspects from a number of angles. He had expanded the design area and was planning to build his own product development area where he would actually make his own prototypes. His experience in Egypt was the catalyst for the project None of his competitors were even thinking along those lines for he was in a league of his own. Michael and Doria would talk over the dinner table and discuss their days…bringing each up to date about their areas of the business.

The company was growing, not only in the domestic market but internationally. Abe had started some tests in Europe and they were relatively successful and Michael felt the time was right to move forward in the fashion capitals of Europe. He sent out his team of real estate people to bring him the best opportunities worldwide. No American retailer had attempted to expand in Europe and Michael was on virgin ground.

- A Cause For All -

"I've been spending most of my day developing the Fall collection. The question is where we want to be on pricing. I tend to overbuild the product line. We definitely want the right looks but we cannot forget the pocketbook of our core customer."

Doria broke in. "Michael, why don't you consider putting together a small collection of better-priced product along with the regular collections? It will serve two purposes, easing us into higher-priced styling and better margin goods."

Michael smiled. "You are now a 'Shmata' person…. I am really proud of you." What's a 'Shmata' person?"

"The best definition is an apparel maven."

"What's a maven?"

"I think we will have to give you a quick education in Yiddish!"

She giggled. "By the way, I have other news worth considering. We are going to have a baby!" Michael was speechless and hugged her.

After many months of an exhausting search, Schmidt finally turned up information that led to Michael and Doria's location. He traced them through his contacts in Egypt that centered on using Doria's mother, who lived in Alexandria, as the source.

Michael had unfinished business in his involvement defeating Nasser and Hassan. He wanted to bring Doria's mother to Boston and enlisted the aid of the Mossad and the CIA. It had taken a lot longer than he expected. Getting his mother-in-law out of Egypt at this time created a political issue. She was literally under house arrest because of Doria. The CIA used its influence with the Egyptian Secret Service to consider allowing Doria's mother to immigrate. It was about to happen when Schmidt was able to get the information he sought.

Both Michael and Doria were excited over Mrs. Sadat's arrival. She would live with them for the time being until they sorted out what she wanted to do.

The pregnancy was going well. Doria wanted to continue to work until almost the day she would deliver. They had decided they did not want to know the sex of the baby beforehand. If it was a boy, Michael wanted to name him David after his father. If it was a girl, the name was open for discussion.

Mrs. Sadat finally arrived. Doria was so nervous anticipating seeing her mother after a three-year period. As her mother exited customs, Doria ran toward her crying. Michael was also there to meet her and the reunion was filled with tears of joy. Even Michael was moved to see Doria so happy and communicating with Mrs. Sadat was not a problem as Michael spoke Arabic.

Mrs. Sadat hugged them both. "I am here in America and I will speak English. My beloved husband, may his soul rest in peace, insisted that I learn English. I am so happy to be away from Egypt. These past months have been so stressful. I have been hounded by the Secret Police daily. Michael, I shall always be in debt to you for arranging my release." She hugged Michael again and all three went hand-in-hand to the car.

"I was allowed to take only one small suitcase as I had to leave everything behind. They ransacked the apartment, taking whatever they wished. I only took things that were precious to me; photos, manuscripts, books my husband had published. I only have one other outfit. I will need clothes."

Doria smiled. "We are in the clothing business, Mother. You need not worry. We will dress you from head to toe."

Michael was also smiling. "May I call you Mother? We want you to feel this is your home, whether you decide to live with us or want your own place. We have lots of time to see how everything works out. In the meantime, you have come at the right time to help Doria with the birth of our baby."

Mrs. Sadat was not the only one who arrived in Boston during these days. Herr Schmidt, with four comrades, touched down one week later. They did not have any issues clearing customs and immigration with their false passports, passing themselves off as businessmen here for a conference and sales meeting.

The plan and the objective were clear. They wanted to kill Michael, Doria, and, if necessary, whoever was in their company at the time. Schmidt and his team planned to do in-depth reconnaissance working out the timing and place of the attack.

Abe had insisted that Michael be under constant coverage by a security force. He had taken the advice of the Mossad who felt there could be repercussions. Cameras were installed in and around the facility and all employees had to present security passes to enter the buildings.

Schmidt's surveillance turned up the following. Michael's main office had two armed security guards at all times. Schmidt did not expect this situation. What he did discover was there was another facility two or three hundred meters away that housed the product development division of the company. Michael would pay a visit to this building daily, generally at the same time each day. There wasn't any security at this site.

Schmidt did not want to have a fire fight with the guards and decided the best way to kill the Jew was to shoot him as he walked to the product development building where he was most vulnerable. If that wasn't possible, he would attack him in the parking lot. Either situation would be close to ideal. The element of surprise was in his favor as he believed Michael was unarmed and would be completely unaware that he was in peril.

Doria was now almost on a half-day schedule as her due date was fast approaching. Schmidt planned to kill her as she exited her car at a shopping center to do her errands, preferably when her mother was along in the car. A two-man team would be responsible for their deaths, gunning them down. It took a few days to develop their plans.

Schmidt wanted to make certain that he and his associates had an escape plan for this was not to be a suicide mission. He had flight plans and a contingency plan to change gears and drive to New York and then fly to Germany. They made a run the day before, including trailing Doria. Schmidt would direct both operations, setting up two-men teams, one team handling Michael and the other team handling Doria. The four men were ex-Nazis and trained SS officers.

Schmidt went about setting up the operation from every angle. He did not want to have to purchase weapons in the States for it would draw attention to the participants. He also didn't know what would be involved. Using the resources of the Odessa, he arranged to ship the weapons needed to Canada and then on to the United States. They arrived in a shipment of machine parts and then were forwarded to a warehouse in Boston where he would claim the shipment. Schmidt relied on the weapons he and his associates had used when they were part of the Waffen SS. They were equipped with Mauser C96 pistols as well as Walther P38, both with 9/X19 m/m specifications. Also in the shipment were Sturmgewehr 44 machine pistols with greater firing power.

Chapter 5

I<small>T WAS EARLY</small> afternoon and Michael, as usual, made his way from his office to the product development center. He passed the security guards with a smile and stopped for small talk. He headed toward the center to see the new prototypes. It was usually the highlight of his day to see his creations come to life. He was already contemplating how he would implement them into the collection.

Schmidt's two-man team was in place. One on foot on the other side of the street, ready to stalk and kill Michael; the other in a van parked further up the street with the motor running, ready to pick up the assassin.

Michael started walking toward the product center. It was a beautiful day and he was in no hurry. He reached for his sunglasses and then decided not to put them on. It was a short walk and he wanted to enjoy the warmth of the sun. Somehow, he turned by accident and noticed a man observing him and keeping pace on the other side of the narrow street. His training by the Mossad had been intense and triggered a sixth sense that spelled danger. His instincts took over but he did not change his pace. In fact, he slowed down so he could change the angle and view the person by feigning looking for something in his pocket. He realized the person, whoever he was, was about to cross to his side of the street.

There were a number of options running through his head. There were cars on either side of the street and a light-colored van was double-parked, idling as if waiting for a passenger. The assassin crossed the street and started to walk faster, cutting the distance between him and Michael. He realized if there was an attack, the man would move against him and then escape with his accomplice in the van.

The killer was slightly confused when he realized Michael was not in view. Michael had stepped behind a parked car and waited for his possible assailant to walk by. The German, now extremely nervous, continued to close the distance. He had drawn his pistol and tried to conceal the weapon under his raincoat.

Michael's instincts were correct as he realized there wasn't any reason to be wearing a raincoat on this day. Michael could see the pistol as the assailant walked by. With a sense of abandonment, Michael launched himself at the killer, as if he were a linebacker, bringing the hit man to the ground. The gunman did not lose control of the weapon and shots reverberated after the fall. Michael grabbed his hand, trying to dislodge the weapon by smashing it against the pavement. They wrestled, both trying to gain leverage. Michael tried to dislodge the assassin's weapon. The killer was extremely strong and finally fell to his knees when two shots caused him to drop the weapon and slump to the sidewalk.

The security guards, hearing the shots, came running and went into action. Michael immediately grabbed the assassin. "Who are you? Why do you want to kill me?" The German had a smile on his face. "Herr Schmidt will kill you and your Egyptian whore."

His dying words made Michael shudder with fear. He looked around as the van sped away. He was in shock and had to reach Doria to make sure she was safe.

Doria and her mother had just arrived at the shopping center. They wanted to purchase some clothing for Mrs. Sadat as she had to leave everything behind when she left Egypt. The mall was quite crowded and parking close to the entrance was not a possibility. They had to look for a suitable space. The second hit team had followed them from their home and was looking for the right situation to do

- A Cause For All -

their work. Schmidt had set up a means of communication between himself and the teams by using walkie-talkies. He had purchased the best equipment he could find that would function within a ten-mile radius of each other. The van driver who fled the scene after his partner was killed finally reached Schmidt. "We could not complete the mission. I believe Fritz is dead and I am fairly sure the target escaped death. He could be wounded."

Schmidt spoke. "You have your instructions. Proceed to the airport and leave."

He immediately called the next team. He did not tell them what had transpired but wanted to know when they would attack. As he put down the walkie-talkie, he was shaking with anger and could hardly contain himself. He feared the worst…total failure. His thoughts turned to self-preservation and his escape plan.

Doria found a parking spot that was not too far from the entrance and was preparing to exit the vehicle. She was going to go around the passenger side to help her mother but she had second thoughts. After living through the escape process in Egypt and Italy, Doria was always very aware of her surroundings. She noticed the same van was always in her rear-view mirror. At first, she thought it was a coincidence but when it started following her around the shopping center, she became frightened but did not want to tell her mother. She decided on a course of action. Just as soon as they entered the parking space, she threw the car in reverse and sped out. The assailants, who were no more than twenty-five feet away, were caught off-guard and opened fire with their machine pistols.

"Mama, get down on the floor as low as possible." Somehow or another, the continuous fire from the automatic weapons did not hit either Doria or her mother. The Land Rover careened off two parked cars in her quest to escape the barrage of fire. She floored the accelerator to avoid the bullets, lost control of the vehicle, and smashed into the cement barriers on the sides of the parking area. The car was moving at over eighty miles per hour on impact. There was a huge explosion. The assailants pulled up to the wreckage and were about to get out to finish their mission when they received fire from an unknown source. Abe Stone, unknown to Michael and Doria, had hired a security company to watch over Doria. Their intervention caused the assailants to cut off the attack and flee. They called Schmidt. "I believe they are dead. They crashed into a concrete barrier, either from our bullets or they lost control. No one could have survived that situation. We could not verify because we were attacked. Proceeding with our escape plan."

Schmidt felt some satisfaction. "At least I managed to kill the Egyptian." His main concern now was to escape. He felt he was safe and unidentified in any way. "I will catch the early Lufthansa flight to Munich tonight and let the others find their way back."

Michael was trembling, unable to comprehend what had occurred, only fearing the words he heard from his assailant concerning Doria. Abe and Sarah were at the offices and rushed out to witness the aftermath of the attack.

Ambulances had arrived for Doria and her mother within minutes of the attack. They were barely alive. Somehow or another, they had survived the attack and the crashes. All three, Michael, Abe, and Sarah, arrived at Beth Israel Hospital, waiting to hear from the doctors. They had received a quick rundown from the security person who saved them from being gunned down after the crash. His gunfire did not allow the assailants to leave the vehicle and shoot them.

Michael's thoughts were at warp speed. "Who did this? He had to be connected to Hassan or Nasser or both. Will this ever end? I will put an end to this madness one way or another. God, save my Doria and her Mom. I cannot endure another loss!"

Hannah and Rachel had now arrived. Everyone was crying and comforting one another, hoping beyond hope. The vigil went on as stillness and sadness settled over the group, focusing on the questions they wanted answered. They were not good at waiting as Abe and Michael paced back and forth without saying a word. Rachel hugged her mother and would not let go.

Finally, the doctor came out. "Mr. Janssen, your wife will live. She has multiple injuries from broken bones to internal injuries. Unfortunately, she has lost the baby, but she will be able to conceive again. Her convalescence will be long and difficult. She will need physical therapy to achieve a recovery. Mrs. Sadat is in critical condition and we will not know the outcome of the surgery for some days. She has sustained multiple internal injuries. We have done everything we can and the next forty-eight hours will tell the story. Both are in the recovery unit. It will be another hour or two before your wife can be seen. For your mother-in-law, it will be longer."

Michael just stood there in shock and, at the same time, thankful that she was alive. Revenge was racing through his mind as he was trying to hold back his anger. He knew he could not let it overtake him as he needed to be in control. Doria didn't know about the baby and this was not the time to tell her. He was concerned about his mother-in-law. What if she didn't make it? The effect of another loss for Doria would be even more devastating. Michael tried to put these racing thoughts out of his mind.

"Your wife can be seen now. Your mother-in-law will need more time before she can be awakened."

Michael went into the recovery room. Doria was a mass of tubes and machines with blue lines fluctuating. Michael was distraught and bent down to kiss her. Doria blinked in approval. She had facial injuries, but they were superficial and would not leave scars. What Michael couldn't see were the internal and psychological injuries that would need months to heal.

Doria did not speak. She was heavily sedated and in the twilight zone. Michael could not bear the thought of telling her about the baby. He just prayed that his mother-in-law did not die. The loss of both would be unimaginable. The doctor and nurse only let him stay a few minutes.

Everyone was waiting for him and were thankful that both Doria and her mother were alive. Michael relayed the extent of Doria's injuries to them. He wanted to wait and be there when she was released from the recovery area and moved into intensive care so he could see her again. He noticed that, when he fought with the assassin, he tore his trousers and bloodied his knee and had some lacerations on his arms. The recovery room nurse also noticed his injuries and had the staff at the nurses' station tend to his wounds.

It was quite some time before Doria and his mother-in-law were brought to the ICU. Michael and Hannah were allowed in and stayed a few minutes. Both seemed to be resting and all you could hear was an array of machines monitoring every possible problem.

Finally, Abe got Michael to go home. "You are exhausted and can't do anything more here. Let's go home. Sarah will make you some matzah and eggs…your favorite. You haven't eaten in ten hours. You need to sleep." Michael passed on the eggs and opted for sleep. He didn't sleep but dialed Bengy in Tel Aviv.

Bengy was his college roommate and a member of the Mossad. He saved Michael's life, putting a head shot into Hassan Streiger who was about to deal a death blow. Michael reiterated the course of events to him. He passed on the information about the statement of the dying assassin. Bengy knew immediately who he was talking about. "Go to sleep. I will meet with Aron and Joshua (who headed the team in the Egyptian operation) and get back to you."

The local authorities wanted to speak with him, and he knew it was necessary to meet with them. They would want to know the 'whys and wherefores'. He needed help and needed to reach the CIA through the Israelis.

Michael's body ached from the struggle with the assassin. He was 'running out of gas'. The adrenaline that drove him was finally subsiding and the reality of the situation drained him in every way. All he could think of was his bride and mother-in-law as he finally fell asleep, fully clothed. There were dreams of the Mossad and how to kill Schmidt. All of this re-occurred, whirling in his head, as he drove to the hospital the next morning.

He had not heard from Tel Aviv. Bengy would reach Aron to get in touch with his people in Virginia to handle the killing. His main concern was his family. He needed to speak with the doctors and get an updated report as to where Doria and Mrs. Sadat were in the recovery process.

Only two people could be in the ICU at the same time. Abe had come along and was with Michael when he spoke with the doctors. "Mr. Janssen, your wife is in relatively good shape in light of what she has been through. The procedure we performed went smoothly. The loss of the baby was a necessity in order to protect the life of your wife. Mrs. Janssen will heal, but it won't be quickly. She was beat up internally pretty badly. She will be in the ICU for at least six days so we can monitor her. We will then put her in a private room.

The doctor continued. "As far as Mrs. Sadat is concerned, she is fighting for her life. We have done all the surgery she can handle at this time; however, we are optimistic she will recover."

Michael acknowledged his report. "I thank you for the information. Whatever needs to be done will be done."

Doria was almost awake when Michael entered. He asked Abe to wait outside for he had to tell her about the baby. They both cried as he held her in his arms. He had sworn an oath to avenge his father's death at the hand of the Nazis. He now swore to avenge his unborn child.

Doria was crying. "Michael, kill them for our baby. Make them pay. Get them for killing our child. Kill them for us and Israel. Kill them!" She asked about her Mom and Michael told her she was recovering and the prognosis was good. He did not want to upset her any more than needed. Michael brought Abe in and they talked for a while.

Chapter 6

TEL AVIV WENT into action immediately. They contacted the CIA, who agreed to contact the local authorities regarding the killing. Bengy, Aron, and Joshua were on a plane to Boston the next day.

When Schmidt found out the attempt on the women was not a fait accompli, he was furious. The entire operation was a failure. He realized that he was now open to retaliation and made plans accordingly.

Michael met Bengy, Aron, and Joshua at the airport. They had flown in on a Gulfstream and went through customs before they left the aircraft. There was a special bond between the four of them. They had been through an experience together that taxed every bit of courage, intelligence, stamina, mental and physical toughness. It created a camaraderie that was there for life. Michael brought them to the conference room. They said hello to Abe and Sarah and closed the door. Michael reiterated the entire story, blow-by-blow. They had lots of questions regarding both murder attempts. The conversation centered on Schmidt. It was sort of a lucky break that the assassin blurted out his name before dying. The boys knew all about him and brought his dossier with them. They had thought he died in the destruction of Hassan's laboratory and facility. He was now targeted, not only by Tel Aviv, but by Michael, who wanted his head.

Bengy broke in. "Michael, don't get excited. Let us handle this. We are well aware of him and will find him."

"You guys don't understand. This is now personal. I want to be a part of the hunt."

"Michael, you are not officially part of the Company. We would love to have you, but you are not trained for this type of operation."

"So, train me!" Michael shouted.

Aron spoke. "Michael, let's be realistic. We will find this SOB and eliminate him and his henchmen. We have personal marching orders from the Prime Minister. We will keep you in the loop and, if we need your expertise, we will not hesitate to enlist your help. You are our expert on Egyptian and Iraqi situations. If that's where he is, we will call. By the way, we didn't come here to see you. We want to see Doria. Michael, there are other events developing that might need your experience level and clout. We may be calling on you sooner than you think."

Michael was reflective for a moment. "I thank you guys for coming. I know you have a busy schedule. Please keep me in the loop and remember I am available to help in any way.

They all went to the hospital together, flowers in hand. Doria was now out of the ICU and in a private room. Michael had a security team there on a twenty-four hour basis.

Aron asked her, "Doria, are you up to telling us what you know about Schmidt? He did come to Egypt with Hassan, as we know from Mr. Nsar. Can you tell us anything about what he did there? Also, do you know anything about his relationship with Hassan? Take your time, we have all day."

Doria smiled. "I do not know much, but here is what I do know. He was Hassan's right-hand man. He had the type of position that had him cleaning up the details and projects that were secondary. There was a feeling that Hassan trusted him with all the details and private information about the business. I really didn't have much to say to him. He spent his time in the munitions warehouse and research facility. He was not a scientist, but he seemed to have technical training. He would do anything Hassan asked…he appeared to be very loyal and was very friendly with the German scientists who were working on the project and staying in the complex. I believe that's all I know." Doria was still full of tubes but in great spirits upon seeing everyone. "I want to thank the Prime Minister for the gorgeous flowers."

They spent close to two hours with her and assured her that the perpetrators would be found and would be eliminated. They all had a special relationship with one another. The attack on Doria and her mother, along with the loss of the baby, made it a personal mission on the part of the three to find Schmidt.

Michael's job now was to nurse Doria back to good health, physically and mentally. He spent early mornings with her before going to the office and then came back in the evening. There was always somebody there. Hannah, Rachel, Abe, or Sarah dropped in during the day along with the security people.

Michael's world was now all about work and Doria. He drove himself relentlessly immersing himself completely in the business. Doria would be at the hospital and then in a facility for physical therapy for quite some time. Michael was, in a sense, living a bachelor's life. The business was essentially his savior. He would go back to the office, mainly the product development facility, after visiting with Doria and work until after midnight. A security person was with him at all times.

Michael would call Bengy every few days for a report on how the search was going. He stayed close to home. All international travel and projects were put on hold for the time being. Abe picked up some of the slack but, in general, the expansion plans were all put aside.

Doria's recovery seemed to be going on schedule. Mrs. Sadat was still hospitalized and slowly but surely gaining strength.

Schmidt knew he had to disappear, at least for the time being, to avoid the wrath of Michael and the Mossad. He knew he had to move quickly. He did not realize that his dead accomplice revealed his identity before dying. Schmidt believed the safest place for him would be in the Middle East. He had met Nasser only once on a trip with Hassan to Egypt. Nasser could possibly use his experience obtaining arms and thought this was his best situation, although he had some ties to government people in Damascus and Iraq.

He tried to reach out to Nasser through the Egyptian Ambassador. Upon hearing of his connection to Hassan, Nasser flew into a rage and conveyed he had no interest in any connection with him.

Schmidt was becoming nervous. He felt the Israelis would be converging on him and his associates and knew that he must move quickly. He turned to his possible connections in Iraq, which were more readily available and willing to accommodate him and his people. He would be in Baghdad shortly and away from danger. If everything worked, he would need help.

His fears were very real as he not only wanted to escape the wrath of the Americans and Israelis, but also had to find a new life. He now had the means to disappear with significant funds and valuable information that was saleable.

Aron and Joshua wanted to find Schmidt, not only for his attempted assassination of Michael and family, but because he was the missing link to Hassan. They suspected there were other elements in the Hassan organization that still existed in one form or another and the key was Schmidt. Was there an armament organization still functioning? Was there an additional connection to Nasser? All of this was now on the table and had to be addressed.

The heart of the Ruhr valley was the industrial area of Germany. The answer was somewhere in this region. They would need to track him and they started in Essen, which was where Hassan's facilities were located. There had to be clues on Schmidt's whereabouts. Most important and what created a sense of urgency was whether Schmidt had the plans for V2 rockets. Did they go up in the explosion or somehow were they in Schmidt's possession? This became a priority and demanded answers.

They knew he would run. The question was where? The natural sanctuary would be Egypt where Hassan had an operation that would fit his expertise. The issue was whether Nasser was willing to give him asylum after the fiasco with Hassan. Mr. Nsar would be in a position to know of his presence.

In the meantime, they started the process at the site of the plant and used their informants for any information. They learned a few things. Schmidt had used the ex-Nazis who had come from Munich and were part of the same organization that Hassan used for his attempt on Michael in Florence, Italy.

In a matter of days, they had zeroed in on four ex-Nazis. They had their names and started to check through their connections to see if they had left the country. They found some sort of trail and managed to find them in Munich. They had little to no information re Hassan's operations. They discovered that Schmidt's plans centered around using the German Embassy in Rome under Herr Mueller, Assistant Director and a member of Odessa.

Aron and Joshua had lost a week in their research, but it was important to go to Boston. Michael needed to see them. They wanted to update him and keep him in the loop.

Aron and Joshua soon eliminated Egypt as their man had communicated that Nasser refused Schmidt's sanctuary. Schmidt only had two other options and was extremely concerned as to where he could hide. What he really wanted was to disappear. There was also an opportunity to reach Argentina. However, since Eichman was captured in 1960 and sent to Israel, he now felt it was unsafe.

Schmidt didn't sit in Germany very long and used the German Embassy in Rome, as Hassan did, for a 'safe house' until his itinerary was finalized.

Herr Mueller, the second in command at the Embassy, was the ex-Nazi who helped set up Hassan's team that attacked Michael and company in Florence. He was part of the Odessa, willing to help any member of the Third Reich. Mueller contacted Damascus and Baghdad to determine the best scenario for Schmidt and, possibly, his henchmen.

Tel Aviv continuously monitored the coming and going of all individuals who visited the German Embassy. Aron and Joshua were now on their way to Rome. They had a dilemma. They did not want to kill Schmidt on Italian soil. The ideal solution was to take him alive. Schmidt was in the Embassy. Why was he there? More than likely, to give him a new identity and send him to the Middle East or South

- *A Cause For All* -

America. The second in command at the Embassy had worked with Hassan and likely hated Israel. He made the plans for Hassan to get the additional people to carry out the assault on Michael in Florence. Could they get to Mueller? That could be difficult but maybe was worth trying. They wanted to avoid an international incident. The best scenario was kidnapping Mueller as he left the Embassy. They were torn as to how to proceed. Taking him alive would clear up many of the questions that were still unsolved in the Hassan Streiger dossier. The chances of achieving their goal were not good.

Mueller had his hands full with Schmidt. He wanted to help him for he was part of the Waffer SS and follower of the Third Reich. He believed the Israelis knew he was in the Embassy and did not want an incident, nor did he want the West German government to realize he was helping an ex-Nazi. There were deliveries of food, linens and materials to the Embassy daily. Mueller arranged for one of these delivery vehicles to be the escape route for Schmidt after all the arrangements had been made.

Schmidt would be going to Baghdad. The plan was to have him depart the Embassy in a delivery van that would drive him directly to Bologna airport where he would board a flight to Paris and connect to Baghdad. He would be using a false identity. This plan would bypass any Israeli surveillance at the Rome airport.

Aron and Joshua realized their chances of capturing Schmidt in Rome were not great. There were too many factors against it. After a week, they left a team there and concentrated their efforts, for the time being, on Schmidt's henchmen. They felt their organization and informants would find his new name.

The main concern was the possibility that Schmidt might have the blueprints for the V2 rockets. There was a distinct possibility this might be the case. The only way to make certain was to capture him! They came up with a number of scenarios. Did Hassan have a set of blueprints in a safe deposit box in Switzerland? Did Schmidt somehow have access? Was there a possibility Schmidt had them?

Chapter 7

MICHAEL WAS IMMERSED in Doria and Mrs. Sadat's recoveries. He was at the rehab center twice a day. He would get to the office at six am, work two hours and head to see them for an hour, then return to the office. He would repeat the schedule at dinner time and then return to the product facility to work late into the night. He needed to be totally occupied to live through this crisis and created a twelve to fourteen-hour day for himself.

Abe and Sarah wanted to curb Michael's impossible schedule. "Michael, you cannot keep working twelve to fourteen hours a day in addition to spending time with Doria. You are running yourself into the ground. You will be of no use to anybody. I do not want to have to visit you and Doria in the hospital. This is madness!"

"Abe, please. I am doing what I must do to keep my sanity. I need to work myself to exhaustion. Otherwise, I cannot sleep. All I think about is Doria, business, and finding those bastards. The order changes by the minute!"

"But, Michael, the boys are on their trail and will find them. We need to leave it to them. They will punish the bastards."

"I know, but that does not make it easier for me. They wanted to kill my beloved. That demands that I personally delve out the punishment."

- A Cause For All -

"I know. Let us take you and the family to Shabbat dinner. Hannah and Rachel want to see you. Let us all take a break."

Michael was driven and his creative juices were at warp speed. He came up with the idea of 'grey goods', being able to color the inventory on what trend was hot at retail. He realized the future of footwear was fashion with the comfort factor and worked with designers to develop comfort constructions that had fashion looks. He felt his product ideas would develop into a wholesale business. He was researching the expansion of casual and lifestyle apparel and footwear. It was a new category and could be the new development. He was burning the candle on both ends and creativity was his savior.

Schmidt's stay at the German Rome Embassy was without issue. The arrangements were made for his departure to Iraq and the trip was confirmed. He was driven to Bologna, leaving the Embassy in disguise, and would take a connecting flight to Iraq.

With his new passport, Mr. Klaus Hoffman boarded the flight to Baghdad, thanks to Mr. Mueller and a three thousand-dollar fee. Schmidt had significant funds above his own as well as access to Hassan's funds which were left in his safekeeping.

The city of Baghdad was founded in the eighth century. It was the center during the "golden age" of Islam in the ninth and tenth centuries, falling to the Ottoman Empire in 1534. It was under the British mandate in 1920 and became the capital of Iraq in 1932 and the Iraqi Republic in 1958, growing to a population of over six hundred thousand.

They drew the map on a political basis, not an ethnic one. Iraq was a twentieth century creation by politicians and statesmen. It was the seat of the oldest and most creative civilization filled with rich resources, the fertile Euphrates valley, the civilization of ancient Mesopotamia and Arab, Islamic heritage. The Turks controlled it for four centuries, using Sunni's as the governing body. The opposition was Arab and Kurds. After the defeat of the Ottoman Five Empire, the British carried out the map of Iraq, formed in 1920, by creating these provinces. The Powers of World War I set up the map, not based on the local population or Iraq's geography, its borders were connected to all its neighbors.

The only unifying factor was the twin river system, which was the lifeline for the agricultural system. The population was totally divided. There were serious demographic divisions in ethnic and linguistic categories.

| Arabic | 75% to 80% |
| Kurds | 15% to 20% |

The Shiite Arabs outnumbered the Sunni minority three to one. The Kurds were Orthodox Sunni and their language was close to Persian.

The British were in control from 1920 to 1932 where they set up a modern government as they did through their Empire. They gave Iraq boundaries, a legal system and dismantled Turkish law. They installed a monarchy in 1920 with King Faisal. The British and the Monarchy prevented any one group from establishing power. The Treaty of 1930 brought Iraq into the League of Nations, opening the door for the withdrawal of the British and the eventual breakdown of the Treaty. In 1933, King Faisal died, causing a struggle for power and resulting in revolt. This led to dominance by the Sunni Arabs.

During World War II, there was a short-lived pro-Nazi government which was defeated in 1941 by the Allied Forces. Iraq was later used as a base for attacks on the Vichy French held by Syria and in support of the Anglo-Soviet invasion of Iran.

Inspired by Nasser's influence, General Qásim overthrew the monarch in 1958, proclaiming an Iraq Republic and rejecting a union with Jordan. There was a military campaign against the Kurds who wanted their own state.

That was the situation in 1965.

The Israelis had a constant vigil watching those entering and leaving the German Embassy in Rome. They now had information that Schmidt had fled there. He was under the protection of Mueller, who headed up the Embassy and was part of the Nazi Elite during the war. As the second in command, he had given Schmidt sanctuary and was working on his escape to Iraq.

Aron and Joshua decided to put the fear of God into Mr. Mueller and see if they could confirm the itinerary of Schmidt. When Mueller left the Embassy for the day and walked to his apartment, Aron and Joshua, disguised as Italian Mafia 'invited' Mr. Mueller for a stroll under the pretext of wanting to know the whereabouts of Schmidt. He and his boss, Hassan Streiger owed them seven hundred fifty thousand dollars and they were not happy. They had bankrolled him on some arms shipments and wanted to have a "discussion" with Schmidt. They were not certain where Hassan was, but Schmidt was alive and they wanted to talk. Mueller, being totally fearful for his life, gave them the information.

Mueller had made the contacts for Schmidt, alias Herr Hoffman. It was the work of the Odessa that had placed his benefactors in Iraq and they welcomed him as part of the community of ex-Nazis.

The boys had their sources in Iraq to confirm his arrival. Photos were sent to Tel Aviv. He was now identified and the focus was centered on Iraq.

Chapter 8

THEY NOW KNEW where he was and brought everyone together to work out the plan. They were fortunate to have a person in Iraq who could be their eyes and ears and do the reconnaissance for them. Their main concerns were: who was he working with and was there a government connection. This information would formulate the plan.

Doria was starting to make significant progress and Michael's spirits soared with her recuperation. It had been almost two months since the incident and Michael felt there was light at the end of the tunnel. Doria's frame of mind was much better and, she was ready to come home. Her mother was also showing some signs of progress. Michael hired a full-time therapist to care for them both. Doria came home first; her mother was a month or two behind.

His schedule really didn't change. The only difference was less travel time. Sarah would be there most days, dropping in around lunch time, keeping Doria company and bringing her chicken soup on a regular basis.

Doria had considerable physical therapy daily and the sessions were showing positive results.

"Michael, as soon as I am better and able to get the OK from the doctor, I want to be pregnant. I need this to happen for us both. We need this baby. We need to be 'whole'. They wrapped their arms around each other.

- A Cause For All -

Schmidt, now Klaus Hoffman, felt secure in Baghdad. In his mind the Mossad had zero presence in Iraq. He now could establish himself with the community. He felt he survived the situations that brought down Hassan and the Egyptian program as well as his ill-fated attempts to kill the Jews. Hassan had called him from Egypt and ordered him to go to his estate, open the safe, and put all the papers in a safe place for his return. He was afraid the Jews would raid and destroy, not only the factory and research facilities, but find all his assets.

Schmidt had gone over the papers and found, to his astonishment, that he had the original plans for the V2 rockets that were developed by the scientists working in the program. Schmidt had not approached a soul or shared this information with anyone. The blueprints were his ticket to a new life, and he was not about to waste the opportunity. He wanted to test the waters and make sure they would go to the highest bidder. Hassan's safe contained a significant amount of U.S. dollars and English pounds, enough to keep him for a reasonable length of time.

Mossad's man in Baghdad felt that Schmidt seemed to be very confident, actually cocky, about his position. He gave the impression to his expats that he wanted to help the cause, the defeat of Israel. He had not made any moves to be involved with the Iraqi regime and, although he was part of the ex-Nazi community, he was guarded. This was the message that was sent to Tel Aviv.

Aron and Joshua didn't know how to read these events for they were now additionally concerned as they felt something was not right. A sense of urgency was now in effect and the lights at the Mossad burned well into the night. They had brought in Bengy, as well as other analysts, to discuss the situation. There were a number of theories on the table. They all centered on what Schmidt knew or had acquired from Hassan. They needed to insert one of their people into Iraq who could find out exactly what Schmidt had that gave him the confidence to feel 'comfortable'.

They reviewed all the information they had compiled as well as the entire Egyptian story. It was a combination of what they knew about Schmidt and everything they had from Hassan Streiger. The problem was the lack of significant information on Schmidt. They were almost certain that he had never met Michael and Bengy. He had seen a photo of Michael but that was the one and only link. That photo of Michael was found on the dead assassin and was not a very good shot.

There was one major question they could not answer. Where were the plans for the V2 rockets that were produced in the Hassan Streiger factory in Essen? Were they destroyed in the explosion? If not, where were they? Did Hassan have a safe deposit box? Are they in Schmidt's hands? These questions had to be answered and the answers were in Iraq.

Michael was sitting in his office when he heard familiar voices talking to Abe in the hallway. He got up from his desk and saw Aron, Joshua, and Bengy standing there.

"What the hell are you doing here? I know you didn't come to see me. It must be to see Doria."

They closed the door. They needed Michael's opinion and expertise on the unanswered questions.

Michael didn't mince words. "Guys, I never got the impression that Hassan would leave the plans in a place where they could be stolen or destroyed. He was too suspicious of everyone. I would bet they were not destroyed in the explosion. My opinion is that Schmidt might have them. If that's the case, he will shop them around. Where will he go? I think we both know the three to four places where they are marketable. So…why are you here? You knew my answer before you arrived."

"You're right!", Aron answered. "We feel we might need your expertise when it comes to an Iraqi issue. Schmidt never met you and has only seen a rough photo. That's what we think. Let's take this a step further and see where it goes. That's enough for today. We are off to see Doria and share a good meal with all of you."

Schmidt was settling into his new home. He realized how fortunate he was to escape the Jews after the plot to kill Janssen and his family. He was not naïve and felt they would be searching for him and may possibly know where he was. He was almost paranoid, thinking he could be kidnapped, as Eichman was in Argentina. He had come upon money when he opened Hassan's safe. Schmidt now had a significant amount of cash at his disposal as well as negotiable securities. Funds were not an issue. He had the V2 blueprints, which were his ticket for asylum and wealth. The ex-Nazi group living in Iraq welcomed him and were more than willing to help him create a new life.

Schmidt had a difficult decision to make. How should he go about selling the blueprints? How should he proceed without exposing himself to possible pressure and harm? Could he insulate himself against the Israelis who want him dead or alive? He needed to formulate a plan to find a buyer who would also guarantee his safety, one way or another.

Michael accompanied the boys on their visit to see Doria. She was excited to see them but immediately asked why they were there. Joshua gave her the explanation. "We had business in Washington and couldn't pass up an opportunity to see you and Michael." Doria smiled. "You Israelis speak with forked tongue." They all laughed. Dinner was fun that evening as it was the first time Doria had been out since the incident. She was her old self and everyone forgot the past for a few hours of camaraderie and joy.

In the morning they convened in the conference room next to Michael's office. "So, gentlemen! I use that term loosely! What's your plan? What are you thinking?"

Joshua started the conversation. "We feel Schmidt has the blueprints and that's unacceptable. They must be either in our hands or destroyed. We think he will offer them to the highest bidder. Schmidt realizes this is going to be a difficult process and he doesn't want to expose himself, yet, he wants the money and possible asylum. We presume this is his situation."

Michael spoke up. "I believe your presumptions are correct. How can I help? I owe this SOB a bullet or capture. Tell me what you are planning."

Aron laid out the plan. "We need to approach Schmidt as brokers making a deal to sell his assets. We haven't finalized how it will work but here is the plan in rough form."

"We need an Iraqi, preferably either a businessman or government employee who would represent the buyer. We would need an ex-Nazi to befriend Schmidt and act as his intermediary. Naturally, the Iraqi would be you, Michael. Bengy, a German-speaking native, would befriend Schmidt and be his person, giving him anonymity. Could it work? There are issues. Michael would need to be disguised. We believe Schmidt really doesn't know what you look like as he has only seen a rough photo. It would not be difficult to change your appearance. The question is: how do we make him aware that he needs Bengy to find Michael and make the deal? We feel we have the ability to scare Schmidt into thinking that he will be seized shortly by the Israelis and get him to move quickly. There are many holes in the plan and we know it needs significant work. The question is: can we persuade you to be that Iraqi? We need you. You have spoken Arabic with an Iraqi dialect since childhood. We know we are asking more than we should, but you are one of us and the element of trust is paramount."

Michael paced the room. "How can I say no? I would give anything to get my hands on Schmidt. I will have a problem with Abe and Sarah and, yes, Doria. It will not be an easy sell."

They broke for lunch and Abe came along. "How was your trip to Washington?"

Aron smiled. "Uneventful."

Joshua re-convened the meeting. "Michael, we feel it will be a two-week operation on your part. Bengy's job will be more involved and there is a distinct possibility that Schmidt doesn't have the blueprints, which means you would not be needed. We should know that sooner rather than later. If you are willing, I would like you to come to Israel when we are ready with the full plan. It will take only two or three days to go over the details. You will then fly to Paris and onto Baghdad with a set of papers and identity. We're asking if you are available for this task by tomorrow. The clock is ticking, and we want to stop Schmidt from disposing of those blueprints. They must not fall into the wrong hands."

Michael thought for a moment. "You will have my answer within twenty-four hours." They continued the discussion, picking each other's brains, for a better plan.

Michael sat at the dinner table with Doria. "Michael, what do they want of you?"

He relayed the whole story to her, leaving nothing out. Doria sat there without saying a word, playing with the silverware. "Michael, do it. Go get the SOB and kill him if you must, but get him for me, for our baby, for my Mom and for Israel. I love you."

He had to speak with Abe, Sarah, Hannah and Rachel and assembled them. "It will be a two, possibly three-week trip. Aron and Joshua will have me go to Israel and then on to my destination. I would not go if Doria was against it, but she realizes what needs to be done and I hope you do too."

They were all crying. "We do not want to lose you, but we know you must do this. Go with God, my son. May the Lord keep you safe."

Michael started growing a beard over the last few days. It would be a necessity. Every Iraqi man had a beard. The rest of the disguise would come from the Israelis. They knew the process.

Three weeks later, he was contacted by Aron and they set up a time for the trip. In the meantime, he set out a business plan to be conducted on his three-week vacation. Michael had been working long hours while Doria was in the hospital and had finished developing prototypes for the coming season. There wouldn't be any missed steps while he was gone. He was rationalizing and he knew it. Michael knew there was more to this than just revenge.

Chapter 9

MICHAEL ALWAYS FELT a special connection upon arriving in Israel. He remembered the first time he arrived and how he became enchanted with the country. It was an instant love story that was now part of his soul.

Aron and Joshua met him as he disembarked and he was led through a special entrance for dignitaries and government officials. His luggage would be picked up by Bengy. They didn't put him in a hotel but instead brought him to a Mossad apartment for the short stay.

In the morning, they got right to work. Fortunately, Michael hadn't suffered any serious jet lag. His beard had grown in very well and he met with the cosmeticians who agreed that, while his coloring was perfect, he needed to look older.

Bengy was already in Iraq and developing his relationship with Klaus Hoffman, aka Schmidt. He had gone to Iraq with an interesting identity. He was an assistant scientist to Dr. Deichmann, who was killed in the explosion at Nasser and Hassan's armament warehouse and research facility. Deichmann was working on the V2 launcher and was well on his way to the finished product. Bengy, now Hans Steiner, was fortunate that he escaped the explosions and the deluge from the water towers. He was not working that evening and was out for dinner, spending the night with his Egyptian girlfriend. Somehow, he heard that someone who had worked for Nitcom, Hassan's company, was living here. One of his German friends helped track Klaus Hoffman down and made the introduction.

Hans Steiner was raised in Dusseldorf and spoke German with a Dusseldorf accent. It was not that far from Essen, just less than an hour train ride. He had found a position with the help of the Mossad person. This person was associated with a technical company that serviced and developed industrial machinery. Bengy was an engineer so he fit in perfectly. He met Klaus Hoffman, alias Schmidt, at the German Club and within a week or two, they were having dinner together two to three times a week. Klaus was pleased to find someone who had worked for Hassan. He actually knew very little of what went on in Egypt and asked Bengy a thousand questions. Bengy was talkative and gave him a complete history of what occurred at the facility. Klaus started to ask him if he had any dealing with the Jew who passed himself off as an importer and buyer of apparel. Bengy thought about it for a moment. "I met him in the dining hall but really never spoke with him. He played chess with the scientists and seemed like a likeable fellow. I couldn't believe who he turned out to be!"

Bengy asked Schmidt. "Did you ever meet him?" "No, never, I have only seen a photo of him and not a very good one."

They seemed to get along quite well and spent more time with one another. Bengy was waiting for the right time to approach Schmidt about anything to do with the aftermath of the explosion in regard to specific information. It was a delicate issue and had to be brought up in the right setting and at the right time.

"Klaus, tell me what happened after Hassan's death and the explosion? Where were you when all this was happening?"

"I was very lucky. I had left the factory an hour before the explosion. I would have been killed. My dearest friend was not so lucky. He died in the explosion."

Bengy hesitated and then spoke. "I am sorry for your loss. We all lost out. My dear friend and fellow scientist, Dr. Deichmann, was killed by the Jews. It was a major loss of a friend and mentor. I would do anything to avenge him."

Schmidt was in rare form and feeling no pain from the schnapps. "I did not let this go without striking back."

Bengy asked softly. "What do you mean?"

"I did my part to strike a blow for all those that were killed. Let's leave it at that. We did not get everything we wanted but it was a blow against the Jews. I wish it was more."

Bengy seized the moment. "Whatever you did, whatever it was, I applaud you. You are a patriot and I am proud to say you are my countryman, a dear friend and part of our national party."

Schmidt was pleased. "I am so happy we found one another and are thinking in the same manner."

Bengy realized this was his opportunity. "Tell me, Klaus, what happened after the loss of Hassan. There must have been lots of things that needed to be looked at. There must have been extremely sensitive material that required decisions. You were the only one to do that."

"My dear friend I will take you into my confidence. I have all the sensitive material from Hassan's company. That includes all the scientific papers and blueprints."

Bengy said softly. "Klaus, let's keep this between us. This is a major development. This material in your hands could be a great benefit and also a grave problem. If you need my help, I believe I can assist you with this situation."

Schmidt was excited. "How can you help?"

"I have possible contacts who could convert this information into a very profitable deal for you and, perhaps, something for me."

Schmidt grabbed his hand. "I would really appreciate if you could help arrange what you are suggesting."

"Klaus, let's not say another word. I will start working on this project. When I have something positive to report, I will give you the details. We need to keep this between us and no one else. We are on dangerous ground. The Israelis are probably looking for you and you need to keep a very low profile."

Schmidt stammered. "I agree whole-heartedly. You are absolutely right."

Bengy gathered the coats. "Let's go home. I will drop you off."

Chapter 10

NASSER HAD TRIED to put the entire Hassan business in perspective. "How had it gone wrong and how did the Jews penetrate the organization in such a way to totally destroy all that Hassan had built? What happened to the intellectual property, scientific information that was in their hands?" He had made a mistake by not bringing Schmidt to Egypt to find out what he knew. Everything was destroyed…Hassan's plant and research facility in Essen and everything in Egypt.

Was there a possibility there were important papers left behind? He brought in his Secret Service team, which included Mr. Nsar, an Israeli spy who had been a key part of the Israeli operation destroying the V2 rocket program. "I want to find Schmidt and bring him to Egypt, whether he comes of his own volition or not. I want him here. Find him!"

Michael was practicing his marksmanship skills as he prepared himself for his trip to Iraq. His disguise had been worked out and was almost completed. Both his hair and beard were gray and heavy. Horn-rimmed glasses were added. His hair was re-styled and the color of his eyes was changed via contact lenses. Even if someone had a copy of the photo in Schmidt's possession, they all felt it would be impossible to identify Michael as the same person.

Michael's cover story was finalized. His new name was Mohamed Samer. He had been in government service and served as an attaché in the State Department in various Middle-Eastern countries over a period of twenty years. He had a diplomatic passport and a regular passport he would use to enter and leave the country. The diplomatic passport would be used to show Schmidt that he had the authority to negotiate.

His new position, after leaving government service, was as an administrator in the same company where Bengy worked, acting as a go-between if there were any government issues. The company was owned by an Iraqi who was a paid informant for the Mossad.

The plan was to have Mohamed Samer be the person who would negotiate a sale, keeping Schmidt and Bengy's anonymity secure. Mohamed was prepared to negotiate with the major countries in the Middle East, outside of Egypt.

The news from Mr. Nsar regarding Nasser's interest in finding Schmidt could be problematic. Michael agreed that this could be a major obstacle. It brought on more pressure to speed up the operation. He communicated daily with Doria and Abe and spoke with Hannah quite a few times before he was ready to go to Iraq.

Bengy felt he had Schmidt under control and sold on what he proposed. He didn't want to press the issue. He had to introduce Michael at the right time. He would be arriving this week and wanted him to get acclimated to his surroundings before the plan was put into effect.

Both Bengy and Schmidt continued to have dinner two to three times a week. Bengy kept the conversation moving, inserting here and there, that a plan was being formulated. Bengy was unsure how to go about discussing the price of the blueprints. It was a tricky situation. He had to feel out Schmidt as to what he considered they were worth.

Chapter 11

NASSER SENT A group of agents to Germany to see if they could find Schmidt. The trail was cold and they were about to give up when they accidently talked to a person in the German Embassy who was recently transferred to Frankfurt. He had heard that Schmidt had been seen at the Embassy in Rome. The trail was still warm as they headed to Italy.

Michael arrived in Baghdad and had no issues passing through immigration and customs. Bengy did not meet him as it wasn't necessary. Michael's accommodations were all confirmed. He was staying in a residence that catered to long-term business people and the lodgings were more than sufficient. He had been speaking Arabic with an Iraqi dialect since childhood and conversing in Tel Aviv in the dialect for about a week. It was a smooth transition. Michael telephoned Bengy and spoke in English with an Iraqi accent with Bengy answering in English-accented German.

Doria was progressing nicely and her goal was to be rid of her crutches and walker before Michael's return. Her mother was finally showing some progress. and Abe and Sarah were still there most lunch hours. They were very concerned with Michael's decision, but it was out of their hands. They could only hope everything would work.

The Egyptian Secret Service team, called the 'Mukhabarat', had a different reception in Rome. The German Embassy refused to give out any information on any German citizen. The Egyptians reported their problems directly to Cairo.

Nasser summoned the German Ambassador to Egypt and asked him for the information on Mr. Schmidt. The Ambassador officially refused and, somehow, a note was sent to the Egyptian Embassy in Rome with Mr. Schmidt's itinerary but not his name on the passport. Herr Mueller, at the German Embassy, decided this method fulfilled the commitment.

A dinner date was arranged for Michael to meet with Bengy and Schmidt. They did not want to push Schmidt too far in the first meeting. Michael was a bit nervous about being recognized. On the other hand, he wanted to strangle him for his attack on his family. Bengy had reserved a private room for the meeting.

"I want you to meet Mohamed Samer, a good friend of mine with special talents that could be helpful to us." They shook hands and sat down. There were pleasantries and small talk. It seemed that Michael passed the identification test with flying colors.

Bengy wanted the conversation to be in German. "Pardon, Mohamed, but I am going to continue the conversation with Klaus in German."

"That's quite all right."

"Klaus, Herr Samer has an impressive resume. For the last twenty years, he has been a part of the Iraqi State Department as an ambassador's assistant throughout the Middle East, serving teams in the Iraqi Embassies in most Arabic countries. He speaks two dialects of Arabic. During his tenure, he has developed relationships with most senior officials who make the decisions. We are very fortunate to enlist his help in working out any programs that are in our interests."

Schmidt was impressed and felt this could be the means to sell his merchandise. They finished dinner and decided they should meet in a secure place to strategize the move forward.

Nasser was enraged when he heard how the German Embassy handled their request. "I want a team to go to Iraq and find this Schmidt and bring him back. Find a way to get it done! I do not want to inform the Iraqi government. This must be handled discreetly. I want him here and I know you can persuade him!"

- A Cause For All -

Aron and Joshua were aware of what was developing with the Egyptians. Mr. Nsar had kept them abreast of what was going on. Aron commented after reading Nsar's last communication. "There is always something you never expect. Michael could be in trouble and someone in the Egyptian group could possibly recognize him. Let's put our heads together and see what we come up with."

Bengy and Michael made plans to meet the next evening. Michael did not know Baghdad and wanted to see the city, not only as a tourist, but also in the event there was a need to escape or lose someone who was following him.

Baghdad was founded twelve hundred fifty years ago. Built as a walled city, the outer wall was eighty feet high with embattlements and a deep moat encircled the outer wall. It was a massive undertaking with over a hundred thousand workers involved in the construction. No other city at that time had developed such a defense. There were four gates with roads that led to the city center. The Kufa gate to the southwest, the Basra gate to the southeast, both opened to the Sarat Canal, which drained the waters of the Euphrates into the Tigris. The other two were the Sham, which led to the desert and Syria, and the Khorasan which was near the Tigris. The four roads were lined with vaulted arcades containing shops and bazaars.

Baghdad was the center of learning and culture from the eighth to ninth century. It linked the trade routes from all directions making the city the road for pilgrims traveling to Mecca. The markets were the most sophisticated and Baghdad was one of the premier trading cities in the ancient world. It's location between the Tigris and Euphrates created the trade link to India and China and, as the population grew, so did the educational and cultural schools. It was the leading center for the Golden Age of Islam. It was revered as the center of the world because of its scholarship and the cosmopolitan breeding ground of knowledge. At the time, the population was over a half million people.

In 1258 it was sacked by the Mongols, a blow from which the Islamic civilization never recovered. It was part of the Mongol Empire for over four hundred years. In 1534, Baghdad was conquered by the Turks and became part of the Ottoman Empire. This occupation lasted over three hundred years and Baghdad remained Turkish with the kingdom of Iraq until the British established control in 1921. Iraq was given formal independence in 1932 and by 1958, under Faisal, the city population was on a path to one million. The sharp increase in petroleum pricing brought about a period of prosperity.

Michael walked the entire city over a three-day period, exploring the center and its economy. The four main roads that ended in the center had countless alleys off each spur. They would hide anyone who wanted to disappear. He now had a working knowledge of the city.

Bengy went to Michael's apartment and discussed how they would approach Schmidt. They did not want to push him but, at the same time, there was a sense of urgency as they had word from Aron that an Egyptian group of three agents would be coming to Baghdad to search for Schmidt within a week to ten days. They wanted to complete the transaction without causing additional problems.

There was a possibility they would have to protect Schmidt and the blueprints from being taken by the Egyptians, which was the last path they wanted to take. Michael thought it was ironic that he wanted to kill this man and, yet, he might have to protect him.

They were curious to hear what Schmidt wanted, monetarily, for the blueprints. Bengy thought it would be quite a price.

Michael felt secure in the city and his ability to speak as an Iraqi allowed him to mingle in the streets, shops, and restaurants for three days using his acquired skills from his Mossad training. He followed Schmidt from his work to see if he had any other 'opportunities' in play. It certainly didn't seem so. Bengy had done his job and sold Schmidt on working with him.

The three-man team that Nasser assigned to the task were waiting for their visas to be confirmed. They made flight reservations, flying from Cairo to Baghdad, hopefully, within the following week. In the meantime, they contacted Iraqi authorities asking them to check all foreigners arriving in the country with a German passport. They expected the information before they departed for Baghdad. They didn't realize that Iraqi government employees work ethics were suspect. They put the request in the pile of requests. The Egyptian

- A Cause For All -

Secret Service would not get this information before they left, nor even when they arrived.

The German Embassy in Baghdad was notified of the Egyptian plans. It wasn't because of efficiency. Any information re German citizens or documents passing through the Iraqi administration were brought over immediately and payment was made upon delivery.

Schmidt was nervous. He feared the Israelis, whom he believed were in the process of searching for him. At the same time, he felt relatively secure in Iraq and was unsure how to go ahead with Bengy. He believed him but was suspicious of the Iraqi, Mohamed Samer. He was under pressure and had to sell the blueprints soon and find a new home. With the funds from the sale, he could find a haven and live in the lap of luxury.

They were asking for a meeting to finalize a plan to reach out to potential buyers. He felt there wasn't any reason not to go ahead with a meeting. How much was it worth? Prices were swimming around in his head.

They all met at Bengy's apartment and Michael could tell that Schmidt was very nervous. Bengy took out the schnapps and they all had a drink.

Bengy led the conversation. "Klaus, we should get this project in motion. Mohamed and I need to see the merchandise that we are going to sell and you have to set a price."

Klaus hesitated. "I have taken photos of the blueprints. Here they are. I will leave these with you, so you have something concrete to negotiate with." They spent a considerable amount of time looking through the photos. Bengy, with his engineering background, felt they were authentic.

Klaus continued. "The key pages, which number 2–3, are missing on purpose. Naturally, they will be included when we have made a deal. We all need protection while negotiating with interested buyers."

Michael commented. "Klaus, I commend you on setting it up in this manner. I believe it is the only safe way to negotiate. Hans and I will have to see the missing pages. I will not negotiate until I know they exist."

Schmidt reached into his briefcase and brought out additional photos. "Here are the images of the missing pages. They are yours to look at here. The original blueprints will only be shown when a confirmed deal is made. I know you understand my need for security."

Michael and Bengy were somewhat surprised but, as they thought about what they were looking at, they probably would have done the same. Bengy examined them and they appeared to be the key pieces.

"I think I would want one of these pages to give the buyer a reason to believe they are genuine."

Schmidt thought about it for a minute. "I agree. Here is an additional page but let us darken the last three paragraphs."

Bengy looked at the photos again. "Klaus, we now need a price and what currencies you are willing to accept."

"I would accept American dollars or British pounds…nothing else." Minimum price is a three-quarter million in either currency. Anything over that is yours."

Michael spoke. "Is the price negotiable?"

"As I said, I want a three-quarter million. I am not interested in your sale price."

They discussed how they would go ahead with selling the blueprints.

Michael was working out the price. "Klaus, I am not sure I can get your price and that does not cover any expenses and commission for us. We need five percent of the three-quarter million to broker the deal and that would be out of the price you are asking. We will go one step further. We will split any overage that we are able to negotiate. If there is none, we expect the five percent from you."

Schmidt started putting the photos in his briefcase. "I understand your position. Let us say, three percent, and we have a deal." "Bengy said, "Done!"

"We will keep you out of the negotiations unless it is absolutely necessary to bring you in. I would not want you exposed…let the buyer think they fell into other hands than yours. You need to find the right country to settle in. The buyer must not know your identity or where you are going." They parted company and agreed to meet in three days to discuss any offers or issues.

In the meantime, Michael and Bengy wanted to discuss their game plan. Schmidt had handled himself very well. His plan was well thought out. He would remain anonymous and would only show prospective buyers just enough to whet their appetites.

Michael smiled. "I didn't think he was that smart. It only goes to show that you shouldn't underestimate your opponent."

Mr. Nsar sent another message to Aron and Joshua. It contained the itinerary for the three Egyptian Secret Service agents as well as their booking information. If the agents got stymied, there was a possibility that Nasser might send Nsar to help. Aron passed on the message to Bengy through their Iraqi contact.

Chapter 12

NASSER WAS TRYING to re-group after the devastating loss of his armament warehouse and research facilities. His armament sources and the entire technical program went up in smoke due to the Israelis. He had very few places to turn in order to replace this much-needed segment of his organization. The answer was Russia. The Soviet Union became the major supplier to Egypt.

During this period, Russian-Egyptian relations were at a high point which resulted in the sale and development of a total Russian weapons system to Egypt.

Nasser was thinking of the possibility of finding the blueprints for the V2 program. Russian technology could resurrect the program and have the weapons to destroy Israel. The downside was sharing the findings with the Russian Bear. The question was: if they had their hands on the information, would Russia have a reason to share with or allow Egypt to use them? He thought the better choice would be to rebuild with German know-how.

All of this was hypothetical as he had to find the blueprints, if they existed at all. He was willing to send his key people to find solutions to many of the issues confronting Egypt.

Michael and Bengy decided they needed to go about this cautiously. Schmidt was under the impression Mohamed was going to contact several countries for the sale. This would take time and they might have to conjure up a whole new scenario. Michael was not sure how this would work but it might need additional Mossad operatives. They needed the originals and had to make sure they had all the copies. It was not an easy task. There were many loose ends that needed to be addressed.

Both started to think about the best and worst case scenarios. They had to prepare for both, while looking at the clock and wanting to finish the work before having to avoid the Egyptian Secret Service.

Schmidt spent most of his free time researching where he wanted to disappear. It seemed the best places were in South America, possibly Brazil, Argentina or Paraguay. There were Germans there and beautiful women. The lifestyle suited him and his money would go far. As soon as the transaction was completed, he would go back to Europe and make plans to immigrate. He needed some expertise and would enlist the aid of Mueller at the Embassy in Rome. Mueller's services were not inexpensive, but he was trustworthy. Schmidt had business in Germany for a day or two and would then travel to his final destination. He had made his usual dinner date with Bengy, and was on his way to the restaurant, one of their favorites.

He was walking on the Basra Road after evening prayers. The city was teeming with bumper-to-bumper traffic, the horns blaring, trying to make their way through the crowds. Schmidt was slowly making his way toward the restaurant which was off the main road in one of a thousand city alleys. The crowds were out buying lamb, vegetables and yogurt, their diet staples. He entered the square and was no more than one hundred meters from the restaurant.

Almost from nowhere vans appeared from different alleys. The doors flung open and Kurdish rebels from the Peshmerga, the military wing of the KDP (Kurdistan Democratic Party) started firing into the crowd.

The word "Peshmerga" originates from the time of the Persian Empire and means "those who sacrifice their lives". They have historically been Kurdish guerillas combatting the ruling power against the Iraqi government over decades.

It was a massacre, bodies falling everywhere, including Schmidt caught in the crossfire. At first, he was stunned and then he tried to run and was cut down on the second wave of fire. There were Iraqi soldiers arriving who rushed toward the ordeal, firing as they ran. The carnage was massive. Bengy had arrived earlier and was standing in the alley near the restaurant, waiting for Schmidt. He stepped back into the shadows and knelt behind a wall.

The Kurds did not stay long. They had done enough damage to make their point. The vans were in the alleys and able to back down and disappear. What they left behind was close to eighty dead and many more wounded.

Bengy ran into the square. He had seen Schmidt approaching from afar. He did not know if he had been wounded or killed. The square was littered with casualties and death. Bengy found Schmidt lying on his back, barely alive. "Stay with me, Klaus. I will get help."

Schmidt was fading and tried to speak. "Hans, get the blueprints from my suitcase I left at...."

"Where, Klaus?"

"My name is Walter Schmidt. The suitcase is at the German Embassy in Rome."

"How do I get it?"

"Ticket in my room."

"Where do you want me to bring it?"

"Herr Adler or my sister." He died on those words.

Bengy took his papers and any form of identification, including his watch. He wanted the authorities to believe he was robbed. He now had his keys and would be able to go to his apartment. All you could hear was the wounded moaning, people screaming and the sound of ambulances arriving. There was total pandemonium as Bengy slipped away. The turn of events put a whole new set of issues before them. Michael was dumbfounded on hearing Bengy recount the disaster.

"God, Almighty, you were fortunate to not have been part of the massacre. One never knows the course of events. I guess we are now about to start a completely new chapter without Mr. Schmidt."

Chapter 13

MICHAEL THOUGHT IT best that Bengy clean out Schmidt's room alone and not cause any added suspicion.

"You should do it soon. Pick the best time when people are not around. We must make sure there is nothing there to identify him or us. Eventually the police will figure it out, but it will take weeks."

"I still can't believe what happened. We should leave and connect with Aron and Joshua. Let them tell us where we should meet. Can you reach our contact here and make it happen? We probably should fly to Paris or London. I know somehow or another we will have to determine how to get the suitcase but let's talk to the boys. This won't be an easy task. There are so many unknown factors. I don't want to think about it right now."

Everyone was excited to hear from Michael. He arrived in London and placed calls to everyone. Doria was overjoyed!" "My dear, I never expected to hear from you so soon. I won't ask how it went. You are safe in London and that's all that matters." Michael spoke at great length with Abe and Sarah and his key person in product development. Hannah was relieved and could not keep back the tears.

Michael wanted to see Sir Arthur Brooks, owner of Fantastique. He was a Siyan, a person who helped Israel in situations of need, and played an important role in the V2 rocket destruction. He actually wanted to discuss some business issues that might be helpful to them both.

"So, Michael, it is always a pleasure to see you. I hope you came here looking for employment. I need you in this organization."

"Thanks, but no thanks. I just wanted to say hello. I'll be here for a few days and wanted to see how you are doing. I have fond memories of being part of your organization." They discussed business in general and Michael was curious as to how he was developing his product facility.

"I am trying to expand ours and hoped you would allow me to see how you had developed yours."

"Of course, Michael…anytime you wish. The new facility is in Spain…you are more than welcome."

Aron and Joshua arrived the following day. They met in Sir Arthur's conference room and went over the entire Iraqi events. Michael's first question was: "Who is Herr Adler from Munich?"

Aron smiled, using a good American expression. "You haven't lost your fast ball. He is not a very nice fellow, to say the least. Herr Adler heads up an organization that wants to build the Fourth Reich. They are called the 'Aryan Nationalist Party', outlawed by the West German government. We do not know that much about him personally. The organization had ties to Hassan Streiger and, I believe, was a supplier to Hassan's projects. Adler was a technical person who, at one time, worked for Hassan's father. The connection between Schmidt and Adler happened in this manner. They were close friends at one time. There was no question Schmidt wanted the money. He could have gone to Adler with the blueprints but it would be impossible to ask him to pay. But, as he was dying, he became "patriotic" and wanted his Nazi bastard friends to have the blueprints. He believed Bengy was one of them and gave him the information. That's how we believe the events occurred. Maybe you have something to add to the story."

Michael didn't say much. "I would like to hear from Bengy."

"Well, Schmidt and I got along from the start. We were both ex-Nazis and lovers of the Third Reich. He was in a bind, fearing the Israelis and possibly Nasser. He wanted to get his money and disappear to Brazil. We offered him that opportunity and, although he was suspicious, he hadn't found another option. He was afraid Mueller, the German Ambassador, would sell him out, probably to the Egyptians. He was terrified of being found. I cleaned out the apartment of everything, leaving absolutely nothing in the room. The ticket for the luggage is here. I would presume it's in the luggage room along with many items left by staff or German Nationals. How we go about that is a separate discussion."

Joshua re-started the conversation. "As far as we know, no one knows of Schmidt's death. Even Mueller has no idea that he is dead. The possibility of his hearing about him is a long shot. There is a good possibility he doesn't even know if he left a suitcase at the Embassy. It's a huge facility. We should move on acquiring the suitcase very soon. We have the ticket and need to find out what's the process. More than likely, you would have to show your passport as well as the ticket. We can check that out quickly. I do not believe we will have a problem retrieving the case."

"The question now is what do we do with this Herr Adler? Did Schmidt ever say anything to Adler about the blueprints? We don't know. Bengy, did Schmidt ever mention Adler's name?"

"He never mentioned Adler by name until he was dying. He did mention he had connections in Munich. Schmidt did not dwell on this subject, but I got the impression that the relationship was real and that he was either part of the organization or was personally involved. What bothers me was that Schmidt had a number of copies of the blueprints, full copies, in his room. I was amazed to see them. It leaves a lot to think about. Do we have them all?"

Michael sat back and tried to digest the whole situation. "Where are we in making sure no one, except us, has these blueprints in their hands? The question is: what was the Schmidt-Adler relationship. What did that entail?"

Aron and Joshua wanted to put this topic aside for a moment and develop a strategy to retrieve the suitcase. They felt it should be handled by having a German subject with a valid passport present the ticket with a letter allowing said person to get the suitcase. It would be necessary to find someone who is a German citizen since the Embassy could check on it fairly quickly. Aron had already put this search into play. A letter of permission, written by Schmidt, would accompany the person picking up the suitcase. It seemed this would be the best method of achieving the objective.

It took about five days to coordinate the operation. Herr Joseph Kruger of Dusseldorf appeared at the German Embassy in Rome and went through security and then was sent to the proper office. He presented his passport, the letter from Schmidt and gave them the claim check. The clerk checked all the documents and went back to the luggage room to find the suitcase. He returned with the case. Kruger signed the documents and was given the leather case. It was a slightly over-sized case that looked like it would hold clothing and toiletries for travel. Kruger picked it up, thanked the clerk and left the Embassy.

Bengy, Aron, and Joshua were there. Michael had returned to Boston. He felt his part of the operation was over, at least for the time being.

It was just about a week later when the boys showed up at his door. "You guys again! What the hell is going on?"

Bengy spoke. "Michael, we want you to see the contents of the case. We need your assessment on what we should do."

The suitcase had been packed within a larger case. Michael noticed they had sliced the linings open to check if anything was hidden.

"Let's look at the contents. The only things we did not bring were some clothing which we checked for any information. There are letters and memos from Hassan to him which we will go over with you. We did not find the original blueprints in this case. What we found were Schmidt's notes, actually to himself for the file, outlining the events that occurred when Hassan called and had him open his safe. If you remember, Hassan feared we were going to find all his assets and wanted Schmidt to keep them safe. It was the only person he could trust and who was available."

Bengy added. "When Hassan was killed, I think availability is the key word here, there were no other options at the time. Schmidt had to escape. He brought the original blueprints to where he thought was a safe place…his sister, Greta Schmidt Hirsch, who lives and works in Dusseldorf. The blueprints were, more or less, camouflaged. Schmidt labeled them 'factory blueprints'. We believe they have never been opened and are sitting in her safe, along with other papers from Hassan and, who knows what else?"

He stopped for a moment. "We believe Schmidt had the combination to her safe and actually deposited everything in it without going over the contents with her. We are reasonably sure his sister never knew what he put in the safe. What makes it complicated is that Ms. Schmidt Hirsch is the managing director of Style Haus and lover to Mr. Karl Adler, the leader of the Aryan Nationalist Party and owner of Style Haus. We know all this from the notes and papers found in his room and suitcase. Schmidt had considerable correspondence with Adler but never mentioned the blueprints. His main concern was making a sale. If he had found a customer, he would have contacted his sister to send the originals."

Michael looked at what was on the table.

Schmidt had made an additional three sets of the blueprints. He was ready to deal with whoever was willing to pay. There was correspondence with Adler which tied him to the Aryan Party.

Bengy continued. "My relationship with Schmidt was definitely based on our mutual concern for the rise of the Fourth Reich and the defeat of the Jews. He never mentioned Adler but referred to an organization that would fulfill his wishes."

"The shooting opened up this whole story. I don't know what would have occurred if he had not been part of the massacre. We need to somehow get to all the facts and then act."

Joshua continued the conversation. "We now have done a complete study on Adler. He had a business relationship with Hassan as a supplier of chemicals and hardware for his projects. The bottom line is that Adler, with his company, has the capacity to build V2 rockets if the blueprints are in his hands. In a way, his technical facilities are as good, possibly better, than Hassan's."

Aron looked at Michael. "I know what you are thinking but we just can't keep blowing up buildings in Germany."

All of this material came into Schmidt's possession when Hassan called, worried that all his papers and financials in his home and safe would fall into Israeli hands. He gave Schmidt the codes to open the safe and hold it for him.

What did Schmidt do with this information? We do not know how or if he dispensed it at all. We feel he did not. Otherwise, he would not be able to sell the important pieces which Bengy has verified."

In recapping all the points, we presume Schmidt, when Hassan called him to open his safe, took all the papers, not knowing what was there. He had plans to bring them to Adler but, after seeing what he had in his hands, he envisioned a sales plan and a solution to all his problems. We do know Adler has the ability to build rockets. We do not think he has plans or prototypes. There is too much we don't know, and that is the problem. How do we go about getting this information? That's our dilemma."

Michael took it all in. "What do you want from me?"

Joshua spoke first. "Adler is a so-called entrepreneur. He is involved in a number of businesses, one of which is the largest low-price women's retail chain in Germany, Style Haus. It is run by his son, who is Nazi through and through, loyal to the cause. He is also a religious fanatic, sort of a strange combination. The son, Heinz Adler, had the title of CEO, but the actual power at Style Haus is Schmidt's sister, Greta Schmidt Hirsch. She is a seasoned retailer and has a very good reputation in the trade. So, my friend, you can see why we are here. You have lived a similar story with Hassan. We need your input."

"These are, in a sense, different circumstances and, at the same time, similar. We debated whether to bring you back into the situation. There are some very difficult issues. Very few people know what actually happened in Egypt. Nasser has downplayed any involvement on the part of Israel and Fantastique. He blames his misfortunes on the accidental explosion. The fashion apparel industry was never really aware of what transpired between Fantastique and Hassan, mainly because Hassan was making bed sheets and had almost zero visibility in the apparel market."

"We feel your know-how in this situation is key. We would like you to consider finishing off this story. As far as we are concerned, it

- A Cause For All -

is still the ghost of Hassan and the arrival of Adler. It needs conclusion! It needs to be put to bed!"

Michael didn't hesitate. "I will help Israel. I just want you to know, as of this moment, I haven't the slightest fucking idea what I can do."

Aron, Joshua, and Bengy were laughing. "Nor do we!"

Chapter 14

THEY SPENT THE rest of the day in Michael's office, outlining all types of scenarios on the blackboard.

It was in the evening that Bengy said, "Let's put this aside and get some dinner. I hope Doria hasn't eaten." They went to Davio's in the Back Bay and, at least for the time being, forgot why they had come to visit.

Michael didn't sleep well, tossing and turning. Doria was up with him and they shared a glass of San Pellegrino. It brought back memories of Italy. They finally fell asleep in each other's arms.

There were two plans that needed to be vetted.

#1   Getting the blueprints of the V2 rockets
#2   Putting Adler out of business.

They discussed Plan One first. "Actually, if we handle this correctly, we can pull this off. Just like any professional thief or safecracker, we have the combination. All we have to do is make sure we are there at the right time. You know the rule: DON'T GET CAUGHT! We could replace the envelope with the same. We believe Schmidt used the same envelopes with markings as he had in the suitcase. Even if they are slightly different, no one has bothered to look at them. All we need to do is work out the timing."

"Adler's operations are housed in Dusseldorf. All the buyers and store administrators are there. The executive and financial offices are in Munich."

Dusseldorf is the fashion capital of Germany. All the major fashion wholesalers and retailers maintain their operations in an area near the airport. The Konig Alle Strasse is the fashion street of Germany. It rivals Via Monte Napoleone in Milan and the Champs Élysées in Paris. Every major retailer seeks a presence in that area. There are major fairgrounds that house international fairs for clothing, footwear and accessories, drawing buyers from Europe and around the world. It also houses major international and financial businesses within the city limits.

Dusseldorf is the seventh largest city in Germany and situated on both sides of the Rhine. It is the cultural center of Germany with its Art scene. The Altstadt, which is the old town, is a tourist entertainment destination, even for the local population.

Michael had been to the city with Abe and Sarah for the international fashion shows. The three would shop the Konig Alle Strasse to see the latest, not only in German fashion, but what represented the very best in what you could categorize as "wearable fashion". The Germans bought, not only directional innovative looks, but those that were classic and in good taste. Michael was interested in expanding his accessories and footwear collections. The Dusseldorf Fair was the place to see the latest from the Italian factories, which were the major suppliers to the German and European markets.

They moved quickly to retrieve the blueprints. The Israeli team was already in place with exact replicas of the envelopes they would, hopefully, find in the safe and swap out.

Entering the retail offices was not a problem. Security was non-existent and the professional safecrackers went about their business quickly and efficiently. There was a sense of relief when the envelopes were opened and the contents viewed. Everyone felt the exchange came off without any issues. The envelopes containing the blueprints had never been opened as they were still sealed. Part of the puzzle was complete.

Michael started the conversation. "Our goal is to eliminate Adler and make sure none of the weapons that he might have will ever see the light of day. So, how do you use me? We got lucky and were able to use my story to penetrate Hassan's organization and, ultimately, bring it down. That is not the situation here. His retail operation is in Dusseldorf, far away from Munich where he has his facilities. How can we link them? Is it possible to use my experience to find the answer? My first, and maybe my only, idea is we need to use Sir Arthur and Fantastique to gain entrance."

Michael paused. "We both know that he may call us "mashuganas" again, but he will, more or less, go along with anything we wish. So, we need to go to London and present our plan and listen to his suggestions because we are going to need him to be involved personally somewhere in this plan. I don't like the idea of involving him, but I don't see how it can be avoided. So, here are my thoughts."

They met in Sir Arthur's private conference room and reiterated their story to set the stage for his involvement.

"Sir Arthur, we are here to enlist your service again. Without your help, Hassan Streiger would be menacing our world. He is gone but he has left his legacy which needs to be eliminated. We need your participation once again, possibly in a greater way. We don't know exactly where you'll be involved, but we are depending on you to help us where needed."

Sir Arthur took a moment to respond. "Well, you know I won't refuse you anything within reason, so without knowing what you mashuganas are planning, I say 'yes'. Now, tell me what you want."

"We need to penetrate Mr. Adler's organization and technical facilities. He is the owner of Style Haus. You know the company well. He's not a competitor as they are primarily selling a different price range and customer. He's also the owner of ADM, a business that has the potential to cause harm to Israel as well as the free world. We want you to make an offer to buy Style Haus at a price over market value that's so ridiculous he can't turn it down. The price is predicated on your wanting entrance into this market and your willingness to pay for it. His organization would be the nucleus to building a retail organization worldwide. Naturally, there would be a need for a full audit and study of the business. That information would have to come, not only from Dusseldorf which handles the everyday workings, but from Munich, which manages all the financial and administrative aspects of the business. This would allow us to get a foothold into the workings of his business. In a nutshell, that's what we are after. The initial offer must come from you. You would have a team of Fantastique executives provide due diligence in every area."

"That's where we come in. The offer, as I said, has to be 'over the top' so it would be impossible not to consider it. There would be widespread coverage in the news, not only from the German press but worldwide financial outlets and apparel publications. So, we need to work with you to come up with the offer. Your expertise in this area is far more than ours. We leave this to your knowledge of the process as you've purchased a number of businesses in building Fantastique."

"Gentlemen, I understand what you are trying to achieve. I will do everything in my power to see your plan come to fruition. My financial team will work on a study of Style Haus and come up with, not only its net worth, but its potential. We need to create some excitement and push this from an apparel industry point of view. We need to start 'whispering' regarding what's about to happen. We will need a campaign. My people are more than capable of helping you make this happen. We have done this before so let us put together a plan and outline it with you. You know, this could be fun! I always wanted to be a spy!"

Aron and Joshua had also done their homework. They had a full dossier on Walter Schmidt's sister, Greta Schmidt Hirsch. She was divorced with no children. Greta Hirsch was a fairly attractive woman, very teutonic-looking, around five feet, five inches tall, brownish/blonde hair with an average figure, not overweight but not in prime shape. She knew how to dress and used clothes to enhance her figure. She was the force that drove the business. Adler's son was an administrator and fancied himself a fashion person. Greta made sure her style sense was incorporated into the buyers' mentality and the merchandise that was selected. She knew how to finesse Heinz and keep him at bay for it was not an easy task. Greta had a relationship with Konrad Adler, who really turned over this business to her. Her problem was having to put up with his son. Greta and Konrad were lovers but, from all reports, the relationship was based more on a business than a personal accord. At least, that was the impression of the team.

As far as evaluating the business, that was really left up to Sir Arthur, who was able to assemble estimates on the volume and profitability of Style Haus. He used all his experience and contacts to reach out to the financial and apparel community for their financial numbers and stability. He went about it seriously as if he wanted to purchase the company.

Michael started spending time in the Style Haus stores so he could give his opinion to Sir Arthur. They had Triple A locations and the presentation was extremely well done. He went over their merchandise for quality and pricing and it was exceptionally good for the price points and quality level.

Michael was thinking and then spoke. "She knows what she's doing. I would say they are doing an excellent job merchandising the product and their presentation is outstanding. You have to tell me what the volume and profitability could be…and then I'll give you my opinion."

Aron and Joshua waited to speak. "Let's give you Adler's resume. He has developed a significant business manufacturing precision tools and machinery that he sells around the world. Adler & Company, ADM, has been a supplier to Nitcom, Hassan's company, for some of the hardware needed to manufacture regular production.

Adler was born in 1917 in Hamburg, raised in a military, political family. In 1936, Adler was part of the Brown Shirts, assigned to Munich, and a full-fledged Nazi during the war as part of the Waffen SS serving in Poland, and on the Russian front. We do not know if he committed atrocities as he was not indicted for war crimes. Adler got his break from Hassan's father, giving him initial orders to manufacture and a capital infusion. This was the start he needed after the war. ADM was part of Germany's resurgence into a major industrial power."

"His personal life portrayed a different personality. Adler is divorced and the circumstances were difficult. He was convicted of battering and abusing his wife and lost custody of his children. His ex-wife did not remarry and has no connection with him, nor do his children. As we said earlier, he is involved with Schmidt's sister in a business and personal relationship. They are lovers and seem to get along, at least it looks that way on the surface. He has a violent temper, few friends, and considers himself an expert on any subject under discussion."

"Adler is on the short side, five foot seven, and stocky, somewhat of a Napoleon complex…not the ideal candidate to represent the 'Master Race". Even though he owns a fashion company, he could care less about how he dresses. He is not involved in the running of Style Haus. We believe he inherited Style Haus from relatives. He's a man of few words and appears to be happy being a loner. The opinion of most of his resources is he is very difficult to do business with and, at times, drives an unreasonable deal. All in all, I would say interacting with him on any basis would be difficult."

"He is a Type 2 diabetic, which causes him problems as he doesn't take proper care of himself. His girlfriend tries to keep him on track, at least it seems that way." They see each other mostly on weekends when she comes to Munich."

"Sir Arthur must make the initial contact, then turn over the negotiations to his financial team and negotiators, which will be us."

The Fantastique team started campaigning news leaks to the German press and the European apparel daily publications. They wanted the "talk" to generate lots of inquiries. Sir Arthur involved the British press and the talk throughout the internet and fashion industry was generating everyday articles in the apparel journals and financial columns. No contact had been made with Adler. The boys felt the information had to come from Sir Arthur to Adler. They all felt the call had to come when he was well versed on the offer.

Michael was still doing due diligence his way. He spent additional time in Style Haus to make sure he knew every aspect of the organization. He was in the main store in Dusseldorf, right off the Konig Alle Strasse, looking at the product lines when, all of a sudden, he heard someone speaking to him.

"Sir, I presume you speak English. I would like to know why you have been spending considerable time shopping our store. I have seen you here a number of times, as well as at our store in Cologne. Who are you?"

"I am David Germain, creative director at Fantastique, based in the UK. I shop the world to see what is happening at all price levels. May I ask, who are you?"

"I am Greta Hirsch, head of merchandising and creative director here at Style Haus." Michael smiled. "We seem to be wearing the same hat. It is a pleasure to meet you. You've probably heard rumors, from one source or another, that we are interested in your operation. Why don't we have lunch? I'm sure we both have interesting questions to ask one another."

Chapter 15

"So, tell me David…may I call you David and please call me Greta. I am not into this German thing with the personal and impersonal protocol."

"Well, it seems we both are in similar positions, which makes us, not only product people, I assume, but non-financial people interested in bringing the best and latest saleable fashion to our customers."

Greta answered quickly. "I agree. The product and image of our operations are the most important to me. I am concerned with the profitability, but I feel if I do my job well, that portion will not be problematic."

Michael smiled. "Well, it seems that you have. It's probably the reason why Sir Arthur Brooks is wanting to buy this business."

Greta was quick with the response. "I can understand why in a sense and, in some ways, it doesn't seem that it would be necessary considering the power of Fantastique."

David put his glass down. "I am putting words into Sir Arthur's mouth, but he would probably say that he didn't want to start from square one and would use your business to grow another multi-national chain."

Greta thought about what he said. "Maybe he's right. Maybe we are the right vehicle. That's if there's a desire for us to sell."

David summed up the conversations. "Well, there are a number of reasons, as we both know.

First is money…lots of money if you have the balance sheet.

Second…to grow the business, as I outlined, to a level you could never do without Fantastique. We would allow you to use your creative ability to do things that today are not available to you. Actually, I am speaking out of turn, but we would not be interested unless you were an integral part of the deal. In our estimation, you are the heart and soul of the operation."

"I thank you for your comments. I have put all of my energy into building this business. Mr. Adler, as you know, is the owner and his son, Heinz, is the administrative head of Style Haus, holding the title of CEO. Do you know him?"

David was straight to the point. "We know your worth to the business. The opportunities for you with a sale are unlimited. It only depends on your ability and willingness to be a team player."

They seemed to get along and, as they spoke, were comfortable with one another. Greta asked Michael about Fantastique and his position.

"Well, I have been with the company forever, working there since I was a school boy. Somehow or another, Sir Arthur discovered me, sent me to school in the States for over six years and then gave me the opportunity to run Product Development." Michael kept it very general. He gave her a brief history of the company as well as some basic facts about the company such as the number of stores. His role in the plan was to sell or influence Greta to be a positive force in wanting Adler to sell the business. Her input could be the deciding factor. They finished lunch and she took him upstairs to her office to show him their latest product developments for the coming season. He was impressed with the merchandise and the style plan. There wasn't any question Michael had scored points. They left it that they should speak and keep in touch on how things developed.

It was time for Sir Arthur to enter into the picture. The next step was to come up with the initial offer which had to come from him.

- A Cause For All -

Greta Hirsch did more than her part. She met Adler the following weekend and reiterated the meeting with David Germain (Michael).

"Konrad, I really liked him, and his approach made a lot of sense. We could get a handsome price for this business and be part of a very progressive company. I know they are willing to overpay to establish a nucleus for a worldwide company. We will not get another opportunity like this in the immediate future. There are very few opportunities out there."

Greta was to the point. "I would like a payday. I have been a babysitter for your son for quite some time, not only teaching him the ropes but putting up with his crap. I really have had it with him. You have expected me to be patient. Well, it's time to change the situation and I believe this would be the right move for us. We both can have paydays. I would not expect you to sell if the offer was not advantageous for all of us."

"My dear, first of all, I have only heard rumors. Talk is cheap. If there is an offer pending from Fantastique, I am here waiting. Why would they want us? They are the most powerful retail chain in the world. They could duplicate us very quickly. I know what you are saying. I don't totally agree with your point of view but, then again, I am really not a retailer. I am concerned about going through due diligence."

"Why is that?"

"Well, we run our business differently. The financials are intertwined with my technological manufacturing business. I am not sure I want the exposure. It's complicated and could be an issue. Fantastique would want a full well-executed audit of our books here in Munich. We could have financial issues that would be difficult to explain."

"I never knew this was a problem."

"Well, it could be, and I am concerned about letting anyone into this facility."

Greta replied. "I need this to happen if the price and circumstances are right. I deserve a payday for building this business and

I want the opportunity to be part of an innovative company for my future."

"What about my son?"

"That will be your problem. Fantastique will not want him; I can assure you of that. You will bring him to Munich."

"He will be a fish out of water there."

"He's your son. You will train him as I did."

"So, tell me more about this Creative Director. You seem to be enamored with him."

"Don't be silly. He gave great insight into Fantastique and its potential. I want to be able to, not only have my payday, but also have the opportunity to create fashion in a growing firm."

"Greta, whoever said you would have a payday? I never stated such a thing."

"Why, you bastard. I would not have taken care of Sonny Boy all these years and fucked you just to have a job. You promised me stability and riches and I have paid my dues."

"Don't get excited. I know what I said, and I want you to have everything you deserve. Let me hear from them and see what their offer entails. Let's not overplay this whole story. This may be a deal that neither of us are happy with. I want to approach this in the right frame of mind. I do not want our personal life involved."

"My dear, that's bullshit! Our personal lives are involved. In fact, they are in jeopardy."

Chapter 16

THE BOYS AND Sir Arthur debated the price. They wanted to quote high but not too high. It had to be in the ballpark and have believability. The price would be discussed in the industry and it had to be based within reason as to the worth of the business. Finally, they agreed.

Sir Arthur picked up the phone and spoke with Adler. "Why don't we meet in Dusseldorf and see if we have something to really talk about? I am not going to ask you for your financials until we have an opening discussion, but we need to meet. I will bring my team along. They will be the people you will work with. So…how about a week from today? We can take a suite at the Breidenbacher Hof so that it will be neutral ground. I am looking forward to meeting you and wishing you a good day."

Adler sat there for a moment thinking about what had just transpired. His English was sufficient but he wished Greta was on the line. He picked up the phone. "My dear, I spoke with Sir Arthur and made a date for us to meet one week from today in Dusseldorf." He reiterated every word he could remember. "So, you have your wish. Let's see if they are serious."

"Adler, they are serious. Sir Arthur would not come to Dusseldorf for a plane ride."

Michael had about ten days before the trip to Dusseldorf. He was pleased with his meeting with Greta and thought his pitch was believable and he had made inroads. They had been more than comfortable with each other. He went back to Boston. Sir Arthur provided his private airplane and also sent some of his staff to visit Michael's operation.

Doria was in great spirits upon seeing Michael. He could see the noticeable improvement in her recovery. She was getting back to her old self.

He sat down with Abe and Sarah and was given a recap of the events. Business was off the charts and inventories were being taxed. The new collection that Michael developed was performing way above plan. Michael wanted to re-order but not in huge quantities. He felt that new product would drive the business. His theory was the customer wanted to see newness in the stores. She would return in four to six weeks and wanted to see a fresh look. The strategy was working. He took the Fantastique people through the operation, glowing in their comments and listening to their suggestions.

Doria and the family went out for dinner and everyone was relaxed, hoping the ordeal was over and Michael was here to stay. He had not yet shared with them what still remained to be done.

Abe came into his office. "So, Michael, don't you think you have done your share? This cannot go on forever. We want you back where you belong, not only developing the business but attending to your life."

"Abe, I have to finish this business. They attacked my Doria and killed my baby. I now know that Adler was a Brown Shirt when my father was killed by these Nazi bastards. It could have been him. Doria wants revenge and I want revenge! I will see it through to the end. I have set into motion a possible conclusion. We have come up with a plan that possibly can work. I need closure and this is the only way it can happen. Please understand."

"I do, Michael. I am just concerned about you. I see the hate and it scares me. I just want you to be at peace."

"I do, too."

- A Cause For All -

Michael took Doria to Vermont. They drank wine and made love. The world was theirs and he felt they were at a point where maybe life had a chance to be normal.

The Breidenbacher Hof was located right off the Konig Alle Strasse and was the premier hotel in Dusseldorf. It had an old-world feel, not so much in the lobby but the rooms were elegant. The suite was perfect for the meeting, large enough with sufficient seating for six people. There was coffee, along with soft drinks, on a side table with an assortment of sweets. All was in order.

The Fantastique contingent arrived on Sir Arthur's plane and made their way from the airport to the hotel. They had to leave London early as they lost an hour coming to the continent. The flight was only an hour and a few minutes as they had the wind at their backs. The team included Sir Arthur, his chief financial officer, Michael and Bengy, with Aron and Joshua rounding up the group. A limousine quickly whisked them away to the downtown.

Adler arrived with his financial person, his son, Heinz, and Greta Hirsch along with an interpreter. Everyone was introduced; Michael, as the Creative Director, Bengy as Chief of Operations, Aron, Joshua and the financial person as the Finance and Administrative heads.

Sir Arthur started the conversation. "I don't want to make this any more complicated or difficult than it should be. We want to buy your business for a fair market price. I won't deceive you. We are willing to pay a premium price so that we can use your organization and build a group of stores throughout Europe and the world without a start-up operation. Style Haus can be the fashion and price tier below Fantastique. We have done a good deal of due diligence in certain areas of your business, principally on the store level. We like what Ms. Hirsch has done merchandising the ranges and your product development fits our style of operation from a timing and development schedule. It is a major point in our assessment of your business.

Adler spoke. "Sir Arthur, I appreciate your coming here and I express my sincerity in your wish to go about this negotiation in an open manner. My English is not perfect. I brought an interpreter just to make sure I am not missing anything. I hope my English is good enough so you understand me."

"You're doing just fine! I want to lay out how we think the due diligence should be conducted so there aren't any misunderstandings. Mr. Germain (Michael), and Mr. Clark (Bengy) will work with your people in Dusseldorf to see how the business works on a daily basis. That entails all phases of administration: all the stores, the buying and styling. They may have reason to go over some of the financial details but that will only be at the domain of the financial people. We know that your financial procedures and records are housed and controlled in Munich. Mr. Simmons, Mr. Fields, and Mr. Clark will be working with your people to confirm the financials and all matters that pertain to the business. I would like to see this done as quickly as possible. We will arrive at a price. It will be based on the following principles:

- 80% will be paid up front
- 15% will be paid after a two-year period with a 5% bonus if all projected numbers are met.

We want you to stay on in this business and this will keep your key people in the right frame of mind. We will arrive at this number together. We have done our homework and believe we will give you a fair price."

Sir Arthur gave them the offer.

Adler gave his comments, this time through the interpreter. "Your plan and offer seem to fit what we expected. I would like a few days to mull it over and give you a decision. There are questions that will arise that I cannot think of at the moment. We need time to digest your proposal. Style Haus has been run by my son and Ms. Greta and I need time to go over everything with them. We will contact you within the week and, if all is in order, start the proceedings."

The meeting, more or less, turned into a social affair. It was time to get to know each other.

Michael did not spend any time with Adler. He gravitated toward Greta and she toward him. "Well, what do you think of Sir Arthur?"

"He certainly is a man who speaks his mind. I personally like his style. We seem to be in the same camp. I would hope that what he laid out seems to be the way it should be handled."

Michael smiled. "I guess we are off to a good start. We both have to be positive forces in this negotiation. I sense that we both are ready to join forces and build a business. It would be a great challenge and be a very new experience for us both. I hope it will also be a great financial win for you."

Greta also smiled. "Well, to be very honest, it has to be if I am part of the venture. I have put my heart and soul into building Style Haus and I am entitled to a financial reward. I am being extremely honest with you. We do not know one another but I know we both are product people who have worked our asses off to build a business. These opportunities very seldom come along and if you don't take advantage when they do, it's your fault!"

Michael nodded in agreement. "Well, you certainly have your head on straight. Let's get it done! I suggest we spend time with one another over the next few weeks if there is a positive answer."

"Don't worry, there will be a decision to go forward."

"You seem certain!"

"More than certain!"

Adler spent some time speaking with Sir Arthur but it was just "small talk" and the group eventually decided to go their separate ways.

On the ride back to London, Michael praised Sir Arthur on his presentation. "You laid it out perfectly. I would expect a positive response as we have a major ally in Greta Hirsch. Her payday is predicated on such a deal. She's in our camp. Now the real work begins. Bengy, Aron, and Joshua are ready to take this to the next level."

Sir Arthur interrupted. "What about the son? He didn't say a word."

Michael chuckled. "He wasn't supposed to!"

Chapter 17

THE EGYPTIAN SECRET Service team had finally arrived in Iraq. They received priority security clearance and used their influence, mainly through Nasser's power in the U.A.R, to get complete cooperation of the State to track down Schmidt. They did not come empty-handed from Essen. There were still remnants of Hussein's company, Nitcom. Some files were still readable after the deluge from the water towers and explosives. They had salvaged a group photo of the executive staff. Schmidt could now be identified.

His body finally was identified with others from the massacre who did not have identification. The police started to check the listings of all foreigners in Baghdad. They did not get far when they received a photo of Schmidt from the Egyptians.

The police were immediately brought in and found almost nothing of consequence in Schmidt's apartment. When the Egyptians identified him, they wanted to see if anything was left and wanted a report from the authorities regarding what happened.

The trail was very cold and the outlook even worse. The police believed his death had occurred because of the Kurdish-led massacre. He had been in the wrong place at the wrong time. There were questions: Was he robbed? That was debatable. Why was his room literally picked clean? There were a number of opinions. Both the police and the Egyptians talked to his employer, who mentioned he had a

- A Cause For All -

friend, a German national, who had worked there until recently. The Egyptians asked if they had a photo of this person. Mr. Hans Steiner seemed to be a close friend and there was a photo with the application for employment.

All this information was brought back to Cairo for analysis by the Secret Service and Nasser. Nasser got excited. "I know this person! He was at the dinner with the Jews as a product production person. There is more here than we know. I want a full report and a dossier on this person as soon as possible. We made a big mistake not seeing Schmidt. What did he want with us and why was he in Iraq? I want to know! Let's put more manpower on this project. I want answers. Maybe it's time we do our own search of what happened at Hassan's factory and see where it leads."

Mr. Nsar was not totally happy that Bengy was put in charge of the operation. He was an Israeli spy and an important cog in Michael's successful plan to eliminate the V2 rockets. However, it brought him into Nasser's constant vision which was not good.

Adler sat down with Greta after the meeting in Dusseldorf. "We have an offer on the table that, on the surface, looks more than promising. I always am suspicious of anyone who wants to pay me more than what I'm worth. It sets off a lot of alarms. I want to know why this is being offered now. I know your answer, but I want to do some research on why this is happening for all the right reasons."

Greta was concerned. "Adler, this is a world-class company, not a run of the mill ill-financed apparel company trying to sell us on a whim! Please, let's not make up something that doesn't exist. On top of this, I am sold on this project. I know this company. It is first class in the apparel industry, probably the number one-rated women's fashion retailer worldwide. First of all, you have zero knowledge of this industry and have zero knowledge of Fantastique. You asked me to run Style Haus and I have done a credible job over the last eight years, bringing you profits and growth. I am voting for this sale and, in fact, I am insisting on it. It is our future. I know it is right and will not take "no" for an answer. Does that tell you where I am in this story?"

Adler tried to be helpful. "Greta, I understand what you are saying. Can I have something to say about this situation? I do not doubt your expertise level and knowledge of the industry, but can I at least have a moment to think about this. I inherited this business by accident. As you know, relatives were going bankrupt and I took it over. I bow to your proficiency and capability. Give me a day or so. "You're right. I will give you your due."

"Greta, my problem is with Heinz. I realize Fantastique will not want him and you have put up with him over the years. We spoke about this before. It is a real problem for me."

Greta replied. "I understand, but not making the sale because of Heinz is a major problem for me…in the business and in our relationship."

Michael waited a few days and then approached Greta. He made a dinner date and they actually ate in the dining room of Greta's hotel. Michael was staying across the street at the Steigenberger. It was an old-world hotel with large, stately rooms. He had stayed there before when he attended the fairs. They met around seven in the evening and had a drink at the table before dinner.

"So, you've had a few days to discuss the possibilities. How is it going?"

"David, I am fairly sold on the idea if the financials work for all of us. I have stated my case with Adler and have said my piece. I am interested in how we would work together. The ability to use the power of Fantastique is really the reason I am pushing this sale. Of course, I want my payday."

Michael commented. "I do not want to pry but do you have a formal agreement with Adler over a sale?"

"No, I do not and, to be candid, I am concerned. It's no secret that we have a personal relationship. There are problems with Heinz Adler which, I believe, you already know. I am concerned…my life has been wrapped up in this business and I am more than anxious if this does not work.""

"Greta, we are always looking for the right people to drive our business. We cannot give you a payday for your years at Style Haus. We are ready to pay you very well and bring you into our organization. Let's have dinner here in the hotel. I think it's the best restaurant in town."

- A Cause For All -

Greta liked Michael. He was good-looking and presented himself extremely well. His knowledge of the industry was exceptional. As Creative Director of Fantastique, his track record had a five-star rating. He seemed to like her and, more importantly, her ability. David was certainly someone she should be close to in every way possible. As dinner was being served, Greta was reviewing the situation and trying to strategize where and what she should be doing. An affair would work for her. She wouldn't push it, but it was definitely a possibility if things worked out. In any case, Fantastique would be an opportunity no matter how it turned out. There were opportunities. The more she fantasized about an affair, the more it sounded exciting. They had another drink.

Nasser was out for blood. He wanted to punish the Jews for destroying his facilities and arms warehouse. The entire V2 rocket project was wiped out.

It was now his mission to find some answers. A five-man team was sent to Germany to determine what had actually occurred. Mr. Nsar led the group. They started in Essen to sift through Hassan's demolished plant to see what they could learn. The key was Schmidt, but he was dead and, as far as they knew, every major executive was killed in the blast.

Nassar had a meeting with the team before they departed. "Who was the Jew that befriended Schmidt? Was he still in the picture? Gentlemen, why was the Jew in Baghdad with Schmidt? He wanted something from him. What was it? The answers are somewhere in Germany. He has to have a history, a family, a girlfriend…something that will give us a lead. Why was the body and room totally clean? Mr. Nsar, I want daily reports!"

Adler really didn't have a choice. If he rejected Fantastique's offer, he was in trouble with Greta, the key to his business. He really didn't like the offer. It was too good, but he felt trapped. It meant bringing his son back to Munich, which, in his estimation, was trouble. He was suspicious and concerned with having Fantastique's financial people in Munich. His financials were intertwined with many other activities that involved manipulation of the tax code. He wasn't looking forward to explaining some of his financial data. The financials were interconnected with his projects. He didn't know if they knew anything about his association with the Aryan Nationalist Party. There was a needed level of secrecy that could not be breached. These projects were too important. This bothered him and he felt a sense of danger in letting Fantastique's team in his facility. They would need to be watched. He was in a difficult situation because of Greta and at a loss on how to handle the problem.

How was he to proceed with developing weaponry under the nose of these Englishmen? He was debating the pros and cons, but finally called Sir Arthur the following day and agreed to go along with the sale. His decision worried him.

Aron and Joshua received the information from Mr. Nsar. It was troubling as they did not need the Egyptians stumbling into their plans. They were depending on Nsar to do his part but that could only be controlled to a point.

Aron was concerned. "I am sure we can control the situation, but it could be a problem for all of us. Nsar can only deflect them so much. We need to consider alternatives. We are off to Munich. Let's see what we can find. We are after the following:

1. Does he have any knowledge of the V2 blueprints?
2. What is he working on that could be used as a threat against Israel?
3. Does he have the ability to develop weapons of mass destruction against us?
4. Is it necessary to kill him?
5. All of the above"

Michael had no interest in getting involved with Greta romantically in any way. He could feel that she was flirting with the idea, but he did not want to develop a relationship with her that would allow them to work together. He felt she had no idea that Adler was wishing to develop weaponry that could brighten the future of a Fourth Reich. She was not a neo-Nazi, at least he didn't believe so. More than likely, he would need her help somewhere down the road to defeat Adler. She and Adler were lovers, but Michael felt it was not a mutual thing. Greta, possibly, used her seduction early on to achieve the position she deserved. She played her cards well with Adler's son and put up with him in order to solidify her position.

No question, it helped to cement her standing for she had the talent, drive, and ambition to, not only run the business, but to build a profitable company. How she felt about Adler now was questionable. She used her position as lover and key employee to reach her goals.

The Egyptians were thorough. They went over every piece of the destroyed site. They talked to the companies that serviced Nitcom. Their search was complete. What they were after were names…people they could talk with about Schmidt, and even Hassan.

The found out that Schmidt's closest friend died in the explosion. Schmidt was not married and, to the best of their knowledge, had no girlfriend. He did leave a sister who was, more or less, estranged. She had not been a part of his life for many years. Was she married? Was she still alive? Did she know anything about Schmidt? As they didn't have her name, they were unable to trace her. They were certain she was not living in Essen or involved or had a real relationship with her brother. Mr. Nsar had to be careful not to obstruct the investigation but, at the same time, he had to mislead them.

Adler, from the first day, was bombarded with questions he had difficulty answering. The Israelis and the Fantastique financial person started the due diligence in Adler's office in Munich. Adler needed an additional experienced, professional financial person to protect his interests. He not only wanted an expert in the field, but needed someone from the Aryan Party whom he trusted. Karl Schneider, a fervent Nazi, was the person Adler selected to oversee the due diligence. He was a lawyer who had extensive experience handling mergers and acquisitions domestically and on an international basis. Schneider was a captain in the Waffen SS and had managed to escape the war crimes tribunals. He came from a Prussian background and a military family. They supported Hitler and the Reich from inception.

When Aron and Joshua heard of Schneider's involvement, they realized his presence could be problematic. What they didn't realize was that he had a connection with Hassan Streiger. Schmidt was the only one available for Hassan to safeguard his property from the Israelis. Actually, Hassan's instructions were for Schmidt to turn over all the papers to Schneider for safekeeping, which never happened. Schmidt realized what he found in Hassan's safe was his ticket to a new life! Hassan and Schneider were working together to further the Reich. Adler was part of the group but did not know the relationship between the two.

Hassan did not trust Schmidt but did not have a choice, He did call Schneider before his death and told him of Schmidt and his papers. Schneider could never track down Schmidt and just let it go. When he heard of Hassan's death and the destruction of Nitcom, he thought Schmidt was killed in the blast. What lingered was the possibility that Hassan's papers were still in existence.

There were opportunities with Nasser and Egypt after World War II for Nazis with security and military credentials. Hassan enlisted the V2 rocket scientists to develop the missiles that would fly from Cairo to Tel Aviv. It was the plan that almost came to fruition. Michael Janssen and the boys from Tel Aviv were able to destroy the rocket programs. Although Hassan was gone and Nasser's plans and facilities were destroyed, the dream and drive was still there!

Schneider was part of that dream. He wanted to know what happened. Why did Hassan and Nasser fail? He knew of Hassan's plans but not the specifics. Schneider had conversations with Hassan which created optimism that the project would succeed. He did not have any connection with Nasser, but he felt he had to renew the German ex-Nazi, Egyptian relationship. Schneider used the West German Ambassador to Egypt to help him develop his relationship with Nasser.

When Nasser dispatched his team to Germany, he asked them to reach Herr Schneider and invite him to Egypt.

Nsar was transmitting this information to Aron and Joshua. Joshua was concerned. "We involved Michael in this operation, thinking he would never be identified. All Nasser knew was he was working for Fantastique. He never knew the facts. He assumed he was a Jew working for Israel. Fantastique denied knowing anything about the situation. They did not publicly make a statement.

- A Cause For All -

Nasser, himself, said nothing. He attributed the facility explosion to an 'accident.'

Aron re-started the conversation. "We never expected to see Nasser or his people involved in this operation. I am worried about Michael's exposure. The only advantage we have is Mr. Nsar in charge of the information given to Nasser. Is that enough to keep him in the game? We must give Michael the facts and discuss the possibility he could be identified by whatever information is passed along to Nasser. The attempt by Schmidt on Michael's life failed. I attribute a lot of that failure to luck on our part and bad planning by Schmidt. That will not happen with Nasser. We have to discuss this with Michael."

When Michael wasn't spending time with Greta learning about Style Haus, he was in Paris to work on his programs and the two prototype boutique stores on each bank of the Seine. Michael's plan was to build a more directional collection. If it was successful, they could start a new division of better-priced merchandise that would be developed in Europe and the major style centers in the States. Their new division would reveal a whole new retail concept.

They met Michael in Dusseldorf. There was dinner at the Steigenberger where they all were staying.

Michael was inquisitive. "How are things going in Munich? I haven't had a chance to speak with you."

"We are just getting started and it looks like it could be difficult."

"Why so?"

"Well, there have been new developments that have changed the situation."

"Tell me."

They reiterated all the information they had discovered since Schneider's entrance into the picture. "Michael, we are concerned about his relationship with Nasser and his possible identification. You know our only contact is your dear friend and compatriot, Mr. Nsar."

Michael was playing with the coffee spoon. "I don't know what to say but it is a real kick in the pants. My first impression is that my contribution is with Greta. I really have no plans to even go to Munich. Why should I even get involved? You guys are leading this program and need to find the information about Adler and his operation. All I am doing is keeping Greta occupied and willing to work with us. I see no reason to be concerned. I am not going to Munich. As far as I am concerned, I am out of the picture. The ball is in your court."

Joshua interrupted. "Michael, you are more than likely to get identified. We cannot guarantee your anonymity."

"Guys, I have to see this through, whether you want to or not. I am involved. It started in Egypt and I think it will probably end there. I don't know how or why but that's my premonition."

Greta and Adler would alternate coming to see each other. Greta did not like going to see Adler in Munich. It was a cold, ill-furnished and sinister-feeling house. The grounds were rather nice, but Munich's weather was unpredictable. She really didn't like to travel. She preferred that he come to Dusseldorf where she had a view of the Rhine and was more relaxed. It was a strange relationship as she always called him Adler.

"Adler, tell me how are you coping with the Englishmen? I hope you are being cooperative. I do not want problems with this deal."

"We are just getting started. This is a complicated negotiation and I have brought on a financial person to help me and my staff."

"Who is he? Do I know him?"

"It's Herr Schneider. I believe you met him a few times at some of our functions."

"Oh, you mean some of your Nazi, Fatherland shit friends that you dragged me to last year."

"It's not shit and I would advise you not to refer to them in that manner."

"Adler, I am not a proponent of anything to do with Hitler or the past. This country seems to be doing very well and I want it to continue on this basis."

"You and I have very different ideas for Germany. Probably the best thing you can do is leave the plans for the 'new' Germany to me and my friends."

"I don't care what you do as long as you don't screw up this deal."

"I am really tired of you lecturing me on what you want and this deal. I can live very nicely without it. I will try to do everything to accommodate you but do not push me too far. I have my limits."

Greta got up from her chair. "And, so do I."

Michael had some decisions to make. Was he going to be a detriment to the whole operation by his exposure? He was torn as to what to do. His relationship with Greta was not an issue. In fact, he felt his presence made her an ally and gave her the courage to be a proponent for the deal. Would he be missed if he bowed out? He thought it would be a mistake to leave. Greta needed support to maintain her position with Adler. In his mind, he still had to be involved.

Aron and Joshua weren't really learning a great deal about ADM and Adler. The financial information was slow in coming. As far as their ability to see the entire operation, it did not materialize. There really wasn't any reason for them to "wander" through their facilities, especially the product development department. They could not duplicate the same situation they created at Hassan's facility in Egypt. A new strategy had to be created! Quickly the lights burned late in Tel Aviv! As far as they were concerned, lightning doesn't strike twice in the same place!

Schneider was not enthused over the sale. Style Haus was a profitable venture and there were no problems with Greta running the operation. He liked the idea that Style Haus could be used as a vehicle for ADM if necessary, using the retail company as a haven to hide funds or create propaganda. He wanted the company to remain in their grasp.

He liked that Adler had very little to do with the business and wanted his son, who was in Dusseldorf, out of his hair. All they had to do was make Greta happy. Schneider thought an equity position in Style Haus would be all that was needed. He was going to present this evaluation to Adler that evening.

"Karl, I like your analysis. I never liked the idea of selling, especially to the English. I will have a difficult time with Greta, but she will get over it. Giving her a partnership should make it easier for her to swallow."

They laughed. Adler went on. "You know we have a relationship. I will go to Dusseldorf and tell her what I have in mind regarding her stake in the business."

Schneider replied. "I would do it quickly and get these people out of your business as soon as possible. First, tell Greta and then call England. It should be done this week."

The Egyptian team felt they had done all they could do in Essen. They did not have a lead on Schmidt's sister. She could not be found. More than likely, she married with a different name or was not alive. They continued to look for a trail. They made plans to meet Mr. Schneider. He could be the person they needed to shed some light on the situation. Schneider was not available for four to five days. They decided they would go to Paris for a holiday.

Chapter 18

GRETA WAS LOUNGING at home when Adler arrived. "Oh, you're early. I didn't expect you until later."

"I just thought I would catch an earlier flight to beat the traffic. I brought a bottle of champagne to toast our new relationship."

"Oh, that's great. I want to hear everything that went on with the Fantastique people."

"Well, there have been some changes."

"I don't understand what you mean."

"The whole deal is off. They initiated a lot of conditions that I just could not accept. I have not told the UK, but as far as I am concerned, it is finished."

"You made that decision without consulting me?"

"Greta, I was concerned for us both. We need our autonomy as well as the methods we use to run our business. The changes they wanted would not work for us."

"May I ask what changes?"

"They were mostly financial concerns, especially as to how we would have to answer to their organization."

"I asked you for specifics. I want to know what they were."

"Greta, their demands were just impossible for us to accept."

"I don't believe you. You are lying. Does your friend, Schneider, have anything to do with this?"

"Darling, no, not at all. I felt this wasn't working out. I have an alternative plan."

"May I hear it?"

"You will be a partner with a twenty percent stake and your salary will be raised by thirty percent."

"I thank you for the offer which you can shove up your ass!"

"Why are you so combative?"

"Combative? You screw up the deal of the century and then come up with an offer that is totally insignificant for the work and results I have achieved. It shows you have really no interest in my efforts and success in running this business. You are a bastard and I cannot believe you would do this to me, considering we also have a relationship. Get the fuck out of here!"

"Greta, wait! Maybe I have been too hasty. Let's sit down and go over this."

Greta went into the closet and started to throw the few clothes he kept there on the floor. "Take your fucking lousy clothes and find yourself another whore and, by the way, another Director of your business. You really don't have a problem. You can let your son run things! I am through as soon as I clean out my office tomorrow."

"Greta, calm done. Let's talk this through."

"The next time we talk, you will be talking to me and my lawyer."

"What do you mean?"

"I have been with you for ten years running your business and licking your cock…I want a payday. We have nothing to talk about."

"Please get your ass out of here and take the champagne!" she yelled as she threw it against the wall.

"Please!"

"I don't want to hear your plan and your story from that financial Nazi prick, Schneider. You both are Nazi bastards and I hope you go to hell."

"You are too excited. I may have been too hasty. Calm down and I will come back later. There is always room for compromise. We have been together a long time."

"Adler, I am calm, and I am in full control of my emotions. I do not want to see you again. It is over…for business and for love. It has been a while coming, but it is time. We will go our separate ways. I want nothing, and I mean nothing, to do with you except to receive a payment for the last ten years. If I do not receive it, there will be hell to pay in every area of your life."

"What do you mean?"

"Adler, I know where all the bodies are buried in your business and personal life. We will settle up and call it a day."

Greta called Michael the next morning. He was in Paris again, working on his project. "Michael, I need to see you. I do not know what has transpired these last hours, but I saw Herr Adler last evening. He has made a decision to back out of the deal. I was firmly against it and gave him my resignation on two counts, personal and business. I would like to see you as a friend and as a mentor as to how to proceed in my business career. I believe Adler's decision is permanent and he will contact Sir Arthur directly. I did not leave my decisions open to negotiation in any way. So, I would hope we are friends and I need one now. When will you be here, or should I go to Paris?"

"I will come. I was about to call you and set up a date. Are you certain about the decision? I would like to give Sir Arthur a call."

"I believe you can do so. The more I go over the course of events, the more I realize that this happened for the best."

Michael immediately called Aron and Joshua in Munich. They were not surprised. In fact, they were relieved for they felt the project was going nowhere.

Aron responded. "I hope he will call Sir Arthur."

"I believe he will. We should meet in London and decide how we should proceed."

Michael made a reservation for Dusseldorf. He was in contact daily with Doria and Abe. He was running his segment of the business as he worked for Israel.

Things seemed to be working out. The test in Paris was progressing well. The prototype stores were in full swing and the upscale collection received an excellent reception. Michael was analyzing the results to see how it would relate to the States. Doria was almost totally recovered and had started working in the administrative end of the business. The new systems she developed were already making a major difference. Abe was ecstatic. His only issue was he wanted Michael back.

Michael didn't plan to stay over in Dusseldorf. He took the early Air France flight with a late return to Paris. Greta didn't want to meet in the office, so Michael made a reservation for a business suite at the Breidenberger Hof.

"Well, Adler called Sir Arthur and gave him a story that centered around a family business that should stay in the family. There was no mention of you, but he wanted his son to be here for his lifetime."

Greta smiled. "Whatever! As far as I'm concerned, he made the right decision and I wish him well. I made it very clear. I do not wish to be involved in his new plans for Style Haus."

"So, my dear, what can I do to help you?"

"You mentioned during our negotiation period that Fantastique would want my services, whether there was an acquisition or not."

"Greta, you have great talent. I would like you involved with me one way or another. There are a number of opportunities on the horizon, all of them interesting. All of them would allow you to use your talents to the utmost. All of them would offer financial rewards. It depends on what and where you want to be. At this moment, that is all I can say. But I assure you, if things materialize the way I would like, you and I will be working together. I am extremely serious making that statement."

"Thank you for having faith in me. We have only known each other for a short time, but I feel I know you and respect your talent and ideas. We seemed to hit it off personally and I am honored to be your friend. Hopefully, someday we will be working together."

Michael smiled. "We are just becoming good friends as I am impressed with your ability and I like your style…no BS. You understand how creative people work and what they need. It is a breath of fresh air. There may be some events that could cause our eventual getting together to seem distant. Things will work out. Let's leave it at that. I know it seems like a strange statement but let's allow things to unfold."

Greta was nervous. "I am not upset or surprised at what you said. I was not born yesterday! I wondered why Fantastique would be interested in Style Haus. I know all the reasons listed were valid. But, when I met all the players, I had a feeling there was an ulterior motive. I don't expect an answer as I know it won't be forthcoming. You gave me your answer and I understand…at least I think I do!" They both laughed.

The conversation turned to the industry, the gossip, and where would be a good place to go for a much-needed vacation.

Michael caught an earlier flight back to Paris.

Chapter 19

ADLER WAS STILL in shock over Greta. He expected a problem, but nothing like what he experienced. He made a mistake and under-estimated her. She was too valuable to the business and, in a way, he loved her. Adler figured he would put together another offer, more money and a thirty percent share. What he didn't understand was that he had burned the bridge. There was no going back.

Schneider consoled him but was actually pleased Adler decided not to sell. He believed there was talent out there that could replace Greta and move the business forward. It was a profitable entity and, even if there were problems, he would still receive a substantial price and not have to reward anyone.

Adler could not reach Greta. She had left Dusseldorf for Miami and parts unknown for a well-needed change of scenery.

The group met in London and used Fantastique's conference room even though the plan would no longer involve the retailer. They had nixed that scenario.

Aron started. "Where are we or are we nowhere?"

Michael jumped in. "I do not think we are nowhere. Let's put all the facts on the board as well as our goals. I think that will help."

Michael scripted the following on the board:

Goals:
- ☐ How to shut down Adler
- ☐ How to solve the problems of copies of the V2 rocket prints. Do they exist?
- ☐ How to stop Nasser's search for information
- ☐ How to contend with Schneider if necessary
- ☐ How not to get caught or cause an international incident

Facts:
- We do not know enough about Adler and Schneider.
- We know what the Egyptians and Nasser are doing.
- We are not sure if there are other copies of the blueprints in existence.
- What is the significance of the contents of the suitcase?
- How can we use Greta and how much does she know?

Joshua added his thoughts as Michael continued to write everything on the board.

1. Let's talk about Greta. We replaced the blueprints in her safe, but we never checked what her brother may have placed there. She is on vacation. I know her schedule. Let's find out what else is in that safe that is of interest to us. That should be done as soon as possible. She is on the "outs" with Adler. I don't know if we can use her against Adler. Let's see how things progress.
2. The blueprints—We are under the presumption we know where they all are. I think the safe will tell the story.
3. We know what the Egyptians know. Is Michael still vulnerable? I believe so. To what extent, I don't know.
4. Adler and Schneider. Adler's company is a source for making weapons of mass destruction. Does he have blueprints? We think not but can't be certain. Schneider, we know, wants to rekindle the relationship with Nasser. Is there a connection with Schmidt or Hassan in some way?

"Let's get something to eat! I'm starved!"

The Egyptian team arrived in Munich after a delightful few days in Paris. They acquired a taste for cognac and were smitten with the women. They had a difficult time getting back "on track". They met Schneider at his office. Nasser wanted information about Schmidt, Hassan, and Schneider.

Mr. Nsar led the discussion as head of the mission. "We were approached by your countryman, Mr. Schmidt, who wanted asylum in Egypt. He was refused because he could not meet the requirements as a scientist or a military person. He mentioned the possibility of having information that would be beneficial to Egypt but was very vague as to what it was. We did not respond, and he disappeared. We could say, he was off the radar. We found him in Iraq just by accident. Since you contacted our President, we thought you might have additional information that could shed some light on the incident. He was an associate of Mr. Hassan Streiger. We also would like to see if you could identify this man who was an associate or friend of Schmidt."

Nsar pulled out a photo that was supposed to be a photo of Bengy, but he had substituted the photo. There was a possibility that Schneider had seen a photo of Bengy from Hassan. "Could you possibly identify this man? It would be a great help."

Schneider looked at the photo. "I've never seen this person."

"Thank you. How can we be of help to you and what would you like us to convey to our President?"

In Mr. Nsar's daily communique with Nasser, he gave a full account of his meeting with Schneider and relayed that no one could identify the photo of the Israeli or friend of Schmidt.

Schneider was ready with his message. "We feel we have the ability to build weapons of mass destruction that could be used to defeat Israel. As members of the Aryan National Party, we are sworn to defeat the Jews, Israel, and all that they stand for. We want Israel destroyed and we want to continue the relationship you had with Mr. Hassan Streiger. This means when we have developed these vehicles, we will bring them to Egypt. We are willing to fund a new research facility in Egypt with German scientists. We want to duplicate the facility and relationship you had with Herr Streiger. I will come to Egypt if Mr. Nasser is truly interested in building this relationship and facility. This is our program going forward. We are in the process of looking for some of Herr Hassan Streiger's development. We believe it still exists.

Mr. Nsar remarked. "Unfortunately, everything was destroyed in Egypt. We were hoping there was significant information still here. Is it possible to meet with Mr. Adler?"

"He will be here at my office shortly. I have made a luncheon date for all of us."

The report that went to Nasser also went to Aron and Joshua.

Michael had the floor. "Greta will be gone at least ten more days. We would like to see everything that is in her safe. We certainly have the time and the means to get this done. We must see this material as soon as possible. I would bet there are surprises there. Schmidt put several items in that safe. We should have seen them sooner. Now is the time!"

Joshua took over. "Thank God for Mr. Nsar. He has saved our asses. We need to figure out how we can use his ability to communicate what we want Nasser to hear. How do we want to handle Adler? They are disasters waiting to happen. What we do not know is what Adler is developing and what he has ready for production. Does he have rocket technology in the pipeline? I believe that is the key issue. I do not want to underestimate this Aryan Nationalistic group. They are well-funded, plenty smart, and dedicated to our destruction. That's not a heathy situation."

"We need to move forward and I need to speak to Tel Aviv. We will need a day, at least, before we forge ahead. Let's get Greta's papers here."

"What are Nsar's plans now? Last, but not least, we do not know for certain what Schmidt did with all Hassan's papers and blueprints. We think we do, but there is room for doubt. I believe what's in Greta's safe will shed more light on our decisions."

Greta was having the time of her life in South Beach, Miami. She felt liberated after her ten-year relationship with Adler. She was just under forty and took fairly good care of herself, working out daily and being somewhat of a vegetarian. She threw caution to the wind, trying waterskiing and screwing everything that had pants. She was totally at ease. Michael had made that happen when he guaranteed her a position with either Fantastique in the U.K. or in the States. Michael actually wanted her to be his second in command in the product development area. The business was growing at a faster rate than anyone could have imagined. He needed Greta's drive, smarts, and ambition for it to continue to grow. She, too, was looking forward to this new life, not really knowing where it would take her.

The contents of Greta's safe arrived and, as Michael predicted, they were full of surprises. They had five days to go over everything before her return. What they could copy without anyone's knowledge was priority.

Hassan's papers created a number of problems. Schmidt had put all these papers in Greta's safe in packages carefully marked "My personal papers. Not to be opened until my death". Greta had no reason to open her safe. She really didn't know or care about what her brother had left in there. They didn't have a very close relationship and only spent Christmas together. Michael had a casual conversation with Greta touching on family and friends. It gave him a good idea of the relationship between sister and brother. Schmidt was two and a half years older than Greta, the only sibling, with both parents deceased.

There were Hassan's documents which included:

- A will leaving his estate to his children and a specific amount of cash to his ex-wife if she outlived him. It was a copy as the original was with his lawyer.
- There was some cash, but everyone presumed Schmidt took most of it with him.
- Schmidt had been busy before leaving for Iraq. He sent out letters and copies of two to three pages of the V2 rocket blueprints to the following. The Red Army factor, known as the RAF, headed by Elsa Goering and based in Stuttgart, Germany.

- *A Cause For All* -

- Eta Basque Separatist Group wanting a country for the Basques in Spain and France.
- The Brigate Rosse in Trento, Italy, a city in the Trentino-Alto Adige region of northern Italy.

He wrote similar letters to each, inquiring if they had any interest in purchasing the blueprints for the V2 rockets. To legitimize his offer, he sent along three pages showing a portion of the blueprints. There were no return letters responding to his offer. They weren't in his room in Baghdad, nor in the suitcase from Rome. They presumed there weren't any answers to his correspondence. Either they were not interested, or Schmidt received a response and destroyed it, which seems unlikely.

Michael was curious. "Was there further correspondence?"

Bengy replied. "There were pieces that I swept up and put in the suitcase, even thrown away notes in his trash, that we couldn't piece together."

Michael said, "Well, now we can. He wasn't sitting around with just us trying to sell his merchandise. Although his first thought was Nasser, he feared that he would either be killed or beaten and sent off because of his association with Hassan." There was correspondence from all three, just pieces. The letters were destroyed. Schmidt just made notes and then disposed of them. I've told you the good news because what it amounts to is that none of these groups have a V2 rocket or anything close. We have no idea what Schmidt sent them for details, but we do have a copy of the photos he sent. We now have a lead; a strange one, but it was the reason why Schmidt reached the Red Army faction in Stuttgart."

"Greta Schmidt went to school with Elsa Goering, co-founder of the Red Army factor. They were best friends in grade school. Here is a copy of the letter Schmidt wrote to the RAF and to her. Schmidt must have known her and enlisted Greta for either a re-introduction or her address, or both. I do not believe Greta is involved. We will know in a few days when she returns from vacation."

Aron broke in. "How do you want to handle it?"

"I'm not sure. I suppose the element of surprise will have to be used in some manner."

Joshua was thinking. "Well, that is the story...not a pretty one. What is making me crazy is how much is out there. And, who has what? Or nothing! Nothing can be taken for granted. What I don't like about all of these organizations is they have had dealings with each other and our dear friend, Abdel Nasser. Anything is possible!"

There was more in the safe.

"All of this is upsetting but the piece that we have not discussed may dwarf all of what we just went over. Schmidt's final correspondence before he left for Iraq was to the Palestinian Liberation Organization outlining what he had sent to the others. We do not know whether there was correspondence between the two. There was nothing in Greta's safe to verify any receipt of any letters. What we did find were addresses and names of people he tried to reach. Did he take those possible replies with him to Iraq and then destroy them? We do not know. We know Bengy found a piece of a document which could be interpreted as correspondence between the two."

The PLO was established in 1964. It's stated goal was the "liberation of Palestine" through armed struggle. The PLO is considered a terrorist organization by Israel and the USA. Their charter only recognizes the boundaries of the British Mandate, meaning there was no place for a Jewish State. Their primary goal was the destruction of the State of Israel.

In 1958, Yasser Arafat and some associates founded Al Fatah, an underground network that advocated armed resistance against Israel. Now this group, under his leadership, had become a full-time revolutionist movement and staged raids into Israel.

"The real threat is Mr. Arafat, another piece of the puzzle that needs to be addressed. This threat, and I call it a threat, is very real as the PLO does not have the ability to make rockets as of now. But, if they had blueprints in their hands, they would find a way to build them or have someone else produce them. We are concerned they are all talking to one another and the results could be disastrous. I feel we have to dissect all this information and see how and where it fits.

On top of this, even though we now know the situation with Nasser, he is probably the greatest threat."

Mr. Nsar and his team returned to Egypt and reiterated their stories to Nasser. He wanted to follow up on Schneider's offer to finance a new facility in Egypt and was willing to bring scientists and technical people to develop a research facility for armaments. A wire was sent to Schneider inviting him to Egypt.

Greta returned from her once in a lifetime "escape", as that's how Michael referred to it when they spoke. They made a date, this time in London. Michael asked her to come there. He needed her on a different playing field.

Michael was surprised! "You look fantastic!"

Greta turned around in her slim-fitting jumpsuit, bronzed and about ten to fifteen pounds lighter. "I could not have had a better time!" She threw her briefcase on the conference table.

"Have you heard from Adler?"

"Oh, yes. He sent me a registered letter outlining his new offer and a legal notification that I had to give him six-months' notice before leaving the position. He said he had a letter I signed when I took the position ten years ago. He did not send me a copy. I have to say the letter was a disgrace. I won't even tell you what is entailed."

"I could have predicted the letter. It's the old story. He gave you your first start so you should work for him as long as he wants you to."

She laughed. "I guess, in his mind, that's how it should be. We had a sexual relationship and that made me his slave."

"I guess so."

"Why am I here? Are you ready to offer me a position?"

"You're here for a number of reasons, that being one of them. I'm torn on how to go forward. In the past four to five weeks, we have become friends. It seems with our views of our industry and ways of doing business, we are sitting on the same side of the table. It has fostered a bond between us that makes me want you to be part of the organization I'm involved with."

"What are you trying to say…that you have changed your mind?"

"Not at all. Just the opposite. I am about to take you into my confidence."

"Please, tell me. I am totally confused."

"When we approached Adler and Style Haus, our objective was to find out all there was to know about, not only Style Haus, but his business and ADM."

"Why?"

"Because we were concerned that Adler was an ex-Nazi and his ulterior motive was to kill Jews and destroy Israel."

"How? Are you an Israeli spy?"

"Not in the truest sense of the word. I am an American. My name is Michael Janssen and I am CEO and Creative Director of a better fashion company, Stone & Co., in the States. I was asked to help defeat the forces that want to destroy the State of Israel."

"I have heard your name. My God, I can't believe this whole situation."

"Why me, Michael Janssen? Is it because I had the experience level to sit down with you and see who and what you are.?"

"To find out if you were involved with your brother. Your brother was working for one of the most dangerous men on the planet. As an ex-Nazi, he found someone with the same political philosophy and became an integral part of the organization. Herr Hassan Streiger sold munitions to all the Banana Republics of the world. Hassan built rockets to reign down upon Israel and his enemies. He wanted to join with Nasser in building a Pan-Nationalistic state. Your brother was part of the plan."

"My brother!. I haven't spoken or seen him since Christmas. If I am lucky, I have nothing to do with his political views and his Nazi bastard friends."

Greta paused. "Wait! I did get a telephone message from him about four months ago saying he was going on a trip and wanted to put some personal papers in my safe along with some other information. He said he could only come on a certain day and I was out of town. He had the combination. He's my only living relative."

Michael started his story. "After Hassan's death, your brother was involved in trying to sell the papers and blueprints of weapons of mass destruction that were developed by Hassan's company. What he did was put all the information that he acquired from Hassan in your safe."

"I am stunned!"

"On top of that, he had you give him the address of your childhood friend, Elsa Goering, who co-founded the RAF. He tried to sell her these weapons."

"Oh, my God!"

"There is more, unfortunately. Your ex-lover, Adler, and his friend, Schneider, are trying to develop the same type of weapons with the help of Nasser. They are in the process of manufacturing these weapons and are about to build a development center in Egypt using German scientists. We need your help to stop all of the projects. We know you are unaware of all that has been going on."

"Let me re-work this in my head. I have questions. Where is my brother?"

"He is dead…not at our hands. He was caught in the crossfire of a terrorist attack in Baghdad and was mortally wounded."

Greta was sobbing. "I am not surprised. I told him a hundred times that he was heading for trouble."

"Other elements may arise that could have connections with Adler and Schneider. You need to keep your ears and eyes open regarding other groups from the Middle East. I am not going to give you every detail but through some luck and our espionage system, we were able to uncover all these events."

"How did you get involved? You're an American?"

"Your brother, angry at the death of Hassan Streiger and because of my involvement in helping Israel, tried to kill me, my wife and unborn child. He succeeded in part. My wife was seriously injured and lost the baby."

"I just can't believe these events."

"Those are the main points of what's transpired. There are other facts, but you now know ninety-nine percent of what occurred."

"So, the buying of Style Haus was just a ploy to get to Adler and destroy the ability to develop the weapons. You had Sir Arthur involved. My God, your guys are incredible."

Greta continued. "Let me ask you some other questions. Where am I in this whole story and, again, what do you specifically want from me? I am being repetitive but bear with me."

"What I have told you is the truth. I am hoping my life goes back to normal and that means you and I are going to be involved in building a business together. I want you to come to the States and learn our business. Depending on how things go, you will either stay in the States or come back here and run the operations we are developing in Europe. That's it in a nutshell."

"Are you only offering me this position because you want me to help you with your espionage?"

"No, I am not...not in the least. Your involvement is up to you. I need your caliber of experience and talent, no other reason. I am not going to chase you around your desk, unless maybe to hug you for doing a great job."

"You won't have to chase me!"

They laughed. "I guess we understand one another."

"Now, let me tell you my thoughts. I do not know what I can do to help, but I am horrified at what has occurred with my brother and Adler. I was just a child when Nazism ruined my country. I will help in any way I can."

"So, let's put our heads together while you're here. I want you to meet some friends of mine. I have to come clean. They have heard our whole conversation."

She thought for a moment. "Oh, one other question. What would you have done if I said 'no'?"

He smiled. "We would have killed you! Let's have lunch."

Chapter 20

Elsa Goering of the RAF Meinhof gang was about to light a cigarette. "I never thought he had the balls or enough intelligence to get involved with Hassan. I knew him twenty years ago. I really didn't know him well. Greta, his sister, and I were close schoolgirl friends and then went our separate ways. Who would have dreamed he would come up with what we received? At first, I thought it was a joke. But, he was serious!"

"I should reach out to Greta and see if he is sane. What he is selling could be interesting, if true. I am not sure if he realizes how dangerous this is. Let's find out."

"Greta runs Style Haus. She has done quite well. As a kid, she was always interested in fashion, and it paid off. I will contact her. It would actually be fun to rekindle a friendship. We did think of dynamiting the Style Haus main store in Frankfurt! I'll call our comrades in Italy and see if they've heard anything. I have a feeling Mr. Schmidt was shopping his merchandise around."

Aron, Joshua, and Bengy didn't ask any questions over lunch. They let Michael lead the conversation, giving the threesome a rundown of Greta's work resume, of which they were already well aware.

Michael laid it out. "This whole situation is very complicated, even for us, in order to keep it in its proper perspective. Let me summarize it for you.

1. There could be responses from the RAF through your girlhood friend.
2. There was correspondence with the Brigato Rosse, a far left terrorist organization, a possibility but not yet a direct link.
3. Adler and Schneider were trying to set up a relationship with Nasser, wanting to build a research center in Egypt to fulfill the plans of Hassan, namely, sending rockets to Israel. We need you to find out their plans and what they are developing.
4. A relationship with the PLO, whose charter advocates the destruction of Israel.
5. The possible interplay between all of these organizations.

Greta, we need your involvement in getting to know the plans of Adler and Schneider. That means getting back to Style Haus. I know what we are asking you is difficult. I don't see any other way of learning what they are up to."

"You are asking me to do something that turns my stomach. You want me to crawl back to that Nazi bastard and sleep with him!"

"If that's what it takes, yes."

They went over the options and filled her in on this history and what they knew about Adler, Schneider, and their relationship to Hassan. Over the years she heard some of the conversations between Adler and his former Nazi associates.

"They meet monthly in Munich. There are fifteen to twenty at these dinner meetings. Every six months or so, they have a social evening and I have been to one or two."

"Can we get a list of the group?"

"I believe I can. Adler is the secretary and I've seen the list of names on his desk."

"I want you to have this number to reach me. If you are in any kind of danger, I want you to call this additional number first. The priorities are to learn what Adler is working on, his plans, and his association with Nasser. Do not take any chances. You are not a spy. Remember that! I am in Dusseldorf the moment you need me. The boys are at your beck and call by dialing that other number. The number one priority is to keep you safe! We don't expect you will hear from anybody else, but it's a possibility. We must know immediately if that happens."

Schneider flew off to Egypt as soon as he received the invitation, but not before meeting with the group and pulling together a plan to present to Nasser. They had similar plans to Hassan and were willing to finance the operation. Would Nasser be willing, after such a horrific loss of face and facilities? He really was their only option that had merit and possibilities. He was involving himself with the Russians, which was a detriment. Communism was always their enemy. It was not clear where this would lead. Schneider was here to analyze the situation.

On his arrival, he was met by Mr. Nsar. "I thank you for the invitation and would like to see how we can work together for our common goal."

Mr. Nsar took over the conversation. "Our President has asked me to show you what he has in mind. I will take you to the old facility that was developed by Mr. Streiger. As you know, the facilities were accidentally destroyed by an explosion. We would like them rebuilt. Shall we go?" Mr. Nsar opened the car door for Schneider and then entered from the other side.

Schneider finally had his audience with Nasser. It was all about money and their ability to staff the facility. "You are developing weaponry. When do you feel you will be ready to bring it to Egypt?

"Depends on a number of issues. I will have a better idea in two months."

"We must get started on rebuilding Hassan's facility. The foundations are still intact. We need to make a definitive plan on how you will proceed. I am more than ready to make the commitment. I would like to hear your ideas and incorporate them into our plans."

"We will send the first technical people when you are ready. When will the funds be available?"

Mr. Nsar was making notes.

Chapter 21

"Greta Schmidt! Do you know who this is?"

"No, you have my private number, so you must be someone I know. Please, I don't have time for a mystery quiz."

"This is Elsa Goering, your childhood friend."

"Oh my God, Elsa! It's been over twenty years since I heard your voice. What do I owe to this pleasure?"

"Actually, I wanted to reach your brother. Can you give me his number? He gave me yours.

"I would, but he is out of the country and I have not heard from him in weeks. Why do you want him?"

"Well, he and I were possibly going to work on a project, and I need his participation."

"I wish I could help you, but I have no idea how to reach him or where he is."

"I am going to be in Dusseldorf next week. How about catching up on twenty years and having dinner? Let's make a date."

Greta could not dial Michael's Paris number fast enough. "Michael, you cannot believe who called."

"I cannot believe how wonderful you look. The years have been good to you." Elsa Goering sat down, facing the street. "Thank you. It has been a long time, hard to believe that much time has passed. You have done quite well running Style Haus. I see your name every once in a while, when the papers mention the retail industry. How's Adler? You know he's a distant cousin."

"I didn't know that. He seems well."

"I really wanted to see your brother as he had tried to reach me. Have you heard from him since we spoke?"

"Not at all, and I am concerned about him. It is not like him to not keep in touch. May I ask what you two were involved in?"

"Just coordinating political stuff. As you know, that's really my business."

"I am not involved at all with anything my brother is engaged in. As I said, I haven't seen him for almost a year."

"Well, you and Adler are close, and he is a far-right supporter and, I believe, one of the leaders of the Aryan National Organization."

"As I said, I'm not at all involved."

"Sounds like it would be difficult not to be on his side."

"You know, Greta, we were great friends in our childhood. I'd very much like to continue the friendship."

"Elsa, you have your hand on my thigh. I'm not into women… sorry."

"My business is totally different than ADM, and the apparel industry has always been leaning left politically. Just the nature of things."

"You are probably right. Thank you for lunch. Let me know when he is back."

"I will. Take care."

She reported the conversation to Michael, emphasizing Elsa was trying to connect her to Adler's organization. "I could not get her to reveal the reason to reach Walter."

Chapter 22

ADLER FELT HE had not only done the right thing by turning the Fantastique purchase down but his position with Greta was solidified. She had capitulated and now his power over her was exactly what he wanted. She was very cool in the bedroom, but that would eventually change. She seemed to want to please him and was far more attentive to his problems and what he was doing in the business. Greta was more than willing to come to Munich. He felt she now realized that this was her life.

"Adler, I want to be more involved with your Aryan organization and your business. We have been together ten years and should not differentiate between our two businesses. I want us to be closer in every way."

Her first task was getting the list of the members of Aryan.

Michael went back to Boston. He felt Greta needed time to mend the fence with Adler. They were hoping for some leads and more information from their sources. Time was needed to let things develop.

Doria was happy to be working and was doing a great job organizing the administrative side. They went away for the weekend and reinvented themselves, walking the trails of Vermont and making love in the early morning hours. Brunch was wonderful…French toast, smothered with apples, cinnamon and real maple syrup.

- A Cause For All -

Michael was not out of touch with the business. Even when he was in France and Germany, he continued to communicate daily through the telex and phone. The time difference worked to his advantage. Abe and Sarah spoke with Michael every day. It seemed they were doing everything right. The new merchandise was more than well-received. The retail plans were performing beyond expectations. Even Michael's experiment in Paris with more directional product was going well.

Chapter 23

WHEN THE PLO received Schmidt's material, they were not sure whether it was genuine or a trap by the Jews. They had business with Hassan Streiger. They had become a problem to contend with for he supplied them with weaponry and ammunition. His deliveries were religiously late and generally filled with merchandise not ordered. They dealt with Schmidt at times who handled their needs.

The political situation was tenuous. The PLO was supposed to represent the Palestinians. In reality, it represented the views of Nasser, who guided the formation of the PLO. Every leader was irresponsible and a puppet of the Egyptians.

In 1965, Yasser Arafat founded an independent Palestinian-run party called Fatah. He had the backing of eighty percent of the Palestinian people, giving them more autonomy from Egypt. The position of the Arab government was that a PLO, under the influence and supervision of the Arab League, could control their political activities. That same year, attacks against the Israeli people escalated under Arafat's leadership.

The opportunity to get their hands on blueprints for rockets would give them the means to strike Israel a death blow. They had been aware of Nasser's rocket development and its demise. If they had the blueprints, their only real course of action would be to go to

- A Cause For All -

Nasser or…could they have any leverage over Nasser's plans in hand? How should they handle the situation?

The ability to create this coup would really solidify his position and assure the Palestinians a new beginning. The decision was made to use any means available to achieve that goal.

The boys from Tel Aviv asked Michael to meet them in London. They needed his expertise on setting the next moves. He had business in Paris, so it fit in with his plans.

Aron began the conversation. "Michael, there are several factors and events affecting our operation that we need to discuss. There are always priorities and unforeseen developments. We're only part of the picture in the whole program to defend Israel and our way of life. We need to bring you up to speed and make some decisions. Let's start with our business. We feel we can rule out any threats from the RAF and the Red Brigade. Schmidt's plans were incomplete, and they never contacted him. Adler and Schneider, to the best of our knowledge, don't have the final plans for the rockets. We believe they could be developed in the long run as they are willing to put a team together to build a research operation in Egypt. In the short term, without the plans, they are not a threat. They're working with Nasser. How that will turn out is unpredictable. We would like to eliminate any effectiveness the Aryan National Party has on our operations and their position in Germany. We are counting on Greta to make that happen."

"What does concern us is what we found in Schmidt's suitcase were blueprints for miniature missiles. They were state of the art, at least on paper. We had our people go over them and learned they were not operational at that point but Hassan did run prototype tests. So far, as an immediate threat, they do not fall into that classification. They seem to be the only ones in existence and they are in our hands. We believe we don't have to address that problem, at least not now."

"That leaves us with the PLO and Arafat. We know they received Schmidt's proposal. We assume, because of his dying words, that nothing transpired. With our informants in that organization, we have a fairly good idea of what they are doing and what they want to achieve. We would like to lead them down a road of our choosing. They would give their eye teeth to acquire the plans, and find a way to produce the rockets. They have Nasser and, possibly, other alternatives. War is coming with Egypt, Syria, and the rest. We need all the advantages we can get! So, Tel Aviv has thrown down the gauntlet to us. How can we use this position to give us an advantage in the impending conflict? You are the genius on Egypt. We want to hear your words of wisdom."

"Michael, before you start, let me bring you up to date on what is really happening with Israel and our neighbors. We need to know the history, the "now". After the 1956 Suez cross, Egypt agreed to the stationing of a UN Emergency Force in the Sinai to ensure all parties would comply with the 1949 Armistice Agreements. Since then, there have been clashes between Israel and the Arabs, particularly with Syria. As you know, in November, Syria consented to a mutual defense agreement with Egypt. The PLO guerillas, under Arafat, widened the conflict by working from the West Bank. We attacked the Jordanian-occupied West Bank village that was the seat of the terrorists. We were admonished by the UN and the United States. Unfortunately, we were engaged by Jordanian troops, which we beat back. King Hussein was critical of Nasser for not coming to Jordan's aid."

The seeds of a conflict were well formed. We believe Nasser is amassing troops in two defined lines…in the Sinai Peninsula on our border and at Sharm el Sheikh, overlooking the Straits of Tiran. There were declarations made in 1957 that any closure of the Straits would be considered an act of war. This prevents shipments to Israel via the Gulf of Aqaba. Nasser has now told the UN peace-keeping forces to leave Egyptian territory. We feel he has been fed information from his Russian advisors indicating this is the time to start a war with Israel. Nasser believes that war would solve Egypt's problems. We know he does not want to face Israel alone. He has approached the Syrians, asking them to shell our positions in the Galilee from the Golan Heights, which they control. He pushed King Hussein to join him. Nasser is on the verge of declaring war, now bolstered by his alliances with Syria and Jordan. That brings us to where we enter the picture. How can we help? Is there a connection that can help us defeat Nasser and company?"

Michael sat back and put his feet up on the table. "Not a pleasant picture, to say the least. My first thoughts are taking advantage of Nasser's hatred of me, Doria, and the destruction of his rockets. He would seek revenge, as did Hassan, at any cost. This is key. We have to find that 'button' to set him off on a wild goose chase that will divert some of his attention to the ensuing conflict. You know the expression…'Don't get mad, get even!' We need to make him mad, and we will get even. Let's put our heads together. I would like all of us to have lunch with Sir Arthur if he's around."

Greta was spending weekends in Munich. "I wonder what you wear to a Nazi get together?"

"Please, Greta. We are late! Can you please get in motion and decide what you want to wear."

"Well, Adler, you look very nice in your new Lederhosen. I know Herr Hitler would be very proud of you."

"Why do you taunt me? You know I am going to get upset and we will argue. I thought those days were behind us."

"You're right. I shouldn't scold you over the past. I'm actually looking forward to meeting some of your friends."

"Please, Greta. Mind your manners. We are expecting some important people this evening from Frankfurt and Hamburg. Some of the parties 'elite'."

"I want to be sure I meet them."

Chapter 24

ARAFAT WAS IN control and his rise was interesting. He was born to Palestinian parents in Cairo, where he spent most of his youth and studied at the university. While a student, he embarked on Arab Nationalist and anti-Zionist ideas. Opposed to the 1948 creation of the State of Israel, he fought alongside the Muslim Brotherhood during the 1948 Arab-Israeli War. Returning to Cairo, he served as President of the General Union of Palestinian Students until 1956. In the 1960's, he co-founded Fatah and operated with several Arab countries. Arafat's words were chilling. "We plan to eliminate the State of Israel and establish a purely Palestinian State. We will make life unbearable for Jews by psychological warfare and population explosion. We Palestinians will take over everything, including all of Jerusalem. The victory march will continue until the Palestinian flag flies in Jerusalem and in all of Palestine."

Aron spoke. "We want Arafat and his people pre-occupied with getting the plans for the rockets. They are suspicious that it is an Israeli trap. We have to change their minds. They only know Schmidt from correspondence or the telex. They never met in person. Our job is to sell them on 'biting' for the plans and meeting with Schmidt or his surrogate. We want him to go to Nasser, plans in hand. At the same time, from our end we have to find a way to antagonize Nasser. I'm not sure how we can do that, but let's throw around some ideas.

- A Cause For All -

Our meeting, or should I say, Schmidt's, should be in Europe, possibly Paris where they have friends. We must send them a credible message. If you want to catch a fish, you have to put a real piece of bait on the hook. They have to believe Schmidt is part of a Nazi organization. We need to get the message to Arafat. First, let's find out where he is. His offices are in Tunisia, so we should send our message there. The particulars have to be worked out. We're not certain what Schmidt asked for a fee. When Bengy and Michael worked with him, it was a half million dollars in pounds or dollars. I believe we should stagger the amount, based on their ability to respond. Actually, it would lend credence to the whole deal. It would also tell them that Schmidt was nervous, afraid of the Israelis or, possibly, the Egyptians who were stalking him. We must come up with a plan for Tunisia as well as Paris. Our next objective is Nasser!"

In 1965, the African Cup of Nations was the fifth edition of the soccer championship of Africa, hosted by Tunisia. It was a good reason for European sports people, as well as worldwide press, to travel there. Tunisia is nestled between Algeria and Libya and the Mediterranean Sea. The name is derived from its capital, Tunis. It has a fascinating history. The country was inhabited by Berber tribes. The coast was settled by Phoenicians as early as the twelfth century. The city of Carthage was founded in the ninth century BC by Phoenicians. It rose to power and became the dominant civilization in the western Mediterranean. Carthage was conquered by Rome in 149 BC, in what we now call a 'Carthaginian Peace', which means a treaty of peace so severe it results in the destruction of the conquered. Carthage was totally destroyed, along with its position in the ancient world. After a series of conquests by the Vandals, the Normans, and Arab rule, the Ottoman conquest took place in 1534, with regime changes lasting until 1957.

In 1869, Tunisia declared itself bankrupt and an international financial commission took control of its economy. In 1881, the French invaded and it officially became a French protectorate and grew to be a major French colony. During World War II, Tunisia was under the collaboration of the Vichy government, which also implemented the persecution and murder of the Jews. After initial defeats, the Allies, with numerical superiority, successfully implemented the Axis Surrender in 1943. Tunisia achieved independence from France in 1956 and declared itself a republic. It was considered one of the most modern, but repressive, countries of the Arab world.

During the championships, two Parisian press reporters came to Fatah headquarters with a communication from their editor to the Director of Fatah or to Yasser Arafat. As they said, their job was just to deliver the material. If they wished to reply, they should contact them at their hotel in Tunis within the next three days. They were only messengers and would take their reply back to Paris.

The package contained a copy of what had originally been sent along with instructions. Also included was a note detailing the amount needed for the exchange of the remaining pages of the blueprints and where and when the transaction should take place. The directions were as follows:

- The meeting place would be Paris.
- The timing would be in ten days.
- The actual meeting would take place at the Cathedral of Notre Dame at eleven in the morning.
- Mr. Schmidt, his associate, or both would be there with the plans.
- If they were able to meet on the earlier date, they would pay four hundred thousand dollars or the equivalent in English pounds. Otherwise, if the meeting takes place on the original date, the price would be five hundred thousand dollars as stated in the original packet.
- A map showing where they would be sitting and information as to what they would be wearing was included. They would be using a code phrase and the reply would be 'Jerusalem'.

Arafat was in Tunis. As he read the instructions, he was debating its authenticity. "It would be quite interesting to be able to sit across the table from Nasser with the plans in my pocket!"

- A Cause For All -

Greta wore a very revealing dress. "Oh, Herr Werner, you are quite charming and I'm so glad we had a chance to talk. Herr Adler has said so many nice things about you. Tell me, what do you really do in this organization? You are an excellent dancer!" Greta moved on to dance with Martin Gruter.

Chapter 25

MICHAEL WAS IN Paris to check on the new prototype stores and work with some resources. He would call Greta within a few days when she had information, but he preferred she called him.

The Arafat plan was moving forward. Tel Aviv had made all the plans for receiving the money. They would give Fatah the missing photos and information. At more than a first glance, it would be the missing pieces. It was short by a point here and there, but it would be like trying to find a needle in a haystack.

Two agents would make the exchange. They would be dressed as priests, sitting in the back of the Cathedral with black alligator briefcases and umbrellas. They would be wearing horn-rimmed glasses. The Fatah people would greet them with the phrase, "What's your favorite city in the world?" The answer would be "Jerusalem".

They would not allow them to count the money, but they could leaf through it to make sure it was all currency notes. The Israelis would have cameras set up to film the carriers somewhere along the way. They felt Arafat would not pass up the opportunity. They were right!

"May I call you Martin? We are all on a first-name basis this evening. I am impressed with your job description. You must be important like Adler. We should dance again soon."

Aron was thrilled! "I am pleased Fatah went for the deal and the early one. We are in the game. The question is will he go to Nasser

- A Cause For All -

or will he try to develop the rockets in Syria, Europe, or bring the Nazis to Tunisia. That's the unknown. Based on his performance in the past, we will be involved with Nasser, second time around. That brings us to Adler and Schneider. Let's call them the Bobsey twins!"

Michael was pacing. "This involves some trickery. Schneider knows Schmidt and probably has been in his company. Our ultimate objective is to get rid of both Schneider and Adler. We need Greta's help. What if she discovered these papers from her brother in her safe but had not heard from him in a long time? She got concerned and opened them up. She didn't know what to do with them, so she showed them to her lover, Adler. It could work."

Michael spent two days with Greta away from her office. She met him in Paris and they shopped the city. It was always fun and a learning experience to walk the Left Bank. They went to Maison Blanche and all of the Saint Germain area. They stayed at the Lutetia, which was once the home of the Gestapo.

Michael liked to shop the major department stores on the Right Bank. Galleria LaFayette and Printemps and had great interest in accessories, shopping the back streets of shoe and handbag shops owned by individual retailers.

If they spoke English, he would pick their brains on what was selling and why. He realized these people "lived" their business and had a direct link to the consumer as to their ideas and preferences. They were a wealth of information. He did the same in the fashion boutiques as well, occasionally buying an item of interest to copy or use as an idea. Greta loved the time with him. It was a learning experience and rewarding.

They mixed business, the strategy of their upcoming charade, with pleasure, which was shopping the city for trends and ideas. They had become good friends and Michael believed in her desire to help them, not only for her business future but to rid the world of these bastards.

Over dinner, they finalized how they were going to proceed. "'Greta, the cardinal rule, which is mine and should be yours, is **don't get caught!** Call the boys! Call us both, but do not hesitate to act if anything becomes difficult…Verstehen sie? When they have the plans and believe they are real, get out!"

Arafat had the plans reviewed by several of his staff members who had engineering and scientific backgrounds. They were legitimate and seemed, for all intent and purpose, to be the original blueprints.

Arafat commented. "So, they are real. I presume our next step is to see how they can come to life as rockets. May Allah be with us."

"What are our options? Are there any others? We know Nasser is more than interested. Could we actually make them ourselves?"

One of the scientists spoke. "The problem is we do not have the components and the necessary machinery to produce one. We do not have the ability to even attempt this project without these components."

It stands to reason. Nasser needed Hassan to deliver the components and the technology. At least some of the technology was his by bringing ex-Nazis to Egypt.

"Our options are limited. I am sure I will get a good reception from the President. Let's make a date with him."

Greta did not give either Adler or Schneider any idea why she wanted to see them. All she said was it was important and extremely upsetting.

"Gentlemen, I was extremely concerned that I have not heard from Walter in over seven months. I tried to reach some of his friends, but no one knew where he was or where he had gone. I know he was terribly upset over the death of Mr. Streiger and the factory explosion. Yesterday I remembered that he called about six months ago and asked if I was going to be in town. He was in a great hurry and wanted to leave some papers in my safe. He was leaving the country on business but did not tell me where he was going. I was going to be away on a store trip, so I told him to use the safe. He had the combination. I never use the safe and hadn't opened it in ages. So, I opened it and what I discovered was incredibly upsetting."

"Well, show us!"

She laid out three envelopes. One contained the blueprints of the V2 Rocket. The others held his correspondence with the RAF and the Basque Separatists.

Adler started to ask questions. "Have you told or shown this to anyone else?"

"Of course not!"

"Are you sure this is from your brother?"

"No one else has the combination of my safe."

"Did you know he had these papers?"

"No! Why are you interrogating me? I came to you for answers. What has my brother got himself into? This is dangerous. I looked at everything and could not believe what I saw. I was thinking of going to the police."

Schneider was stunned. "Please excuse us. We are as amazed as you. This is almost unbelievable. Can you give us any additional information?"

"You know what I know, no more."

Adler looked at Greta. "Greta, I am glad you came to us instead of the authorities. I want you to keep this to ourselves. We have our own sources and will try to find your brother and put these issues to rest."

Greta replied. "I don't want any part of it. I only want to know that Walter is safe and not in trouble. I leave the rest to you."

"My dear, we will do everything possible to find him. Let's all have dinner together."

"I can't stay. We are running a major promotion in the stores this weekend. I need to return on the evening flight. Thank you for taking care of this. I would not know what to do without you."

Greta was trembling as she entered the limousine for the ride to the airport. When she boarded the plane, she went to the restroom and removed the recording device she was wearing.

Chapter 26

ARAFAT AND NASSER got along fairly well since the President was Arafat's mentor and initiated the rise of Fatah.

"So, my friend, how does the battle go with the Jews? You seem to be causing a lot of mischief on the Israelis."

"Not as much as I would like!" He laid the plans out on the conference table.

"Where did you get them?"

He told Nasser the story of Schmidt and their negotiation. "I was foolish to turn him away. He tried to reach me, most likely because of these plans. I was insane over Hassan and the Jews and was out for their blood. Are you certain they are genuine?"

"As far as I know. I have shown them to my engineers and scientific staff. They all agree they are authentic."

"We shall get on this immediately. By the way, where else did you shop?"

"I came to you first. I wouldn't think of not working with you."

"Let me finish that sentence...unless you found someone better equipped."

They both laughed.

Nasser added. "One other point. Do you have any reason to think the Jews are behind this 'find'?"

Arafat was philosophical. "I did, hoping that Allah would not curse us with such a situation. I have German scientists on the way to confirm the authenticity of the blueprints. I am in the process of building a new research center on the original site."

Arafat couldn't help but bring up the debacle of the V2 rockets. Michael, Doria, and Bengy had used the dynamiting of the water towers to destroy the rockets and research facilities.

"Well, don't build it near any water towers!"

"You can be sure of that!", he said, as he rolled up the plans, his hands tightening the cord more than needed.

Chapter 27

THE LIGHTS WERE again burning late into the night as Joshua and Aron were trying to gauge where they were in their strategic plan. They had been in touch with their fellow brethren and were in the midst of trying to interpret the past months. Aron smiled as he read the incoming message from Mr. Nsar. He passed it to Bengy and Joshua.

Adler and Schneider were making plans as to how to approach Nasser. They had no reason to doubt Greta. Everything she said seemed to fit the situation. Schneider knew more than Schmidt. Schneider knew of the contents of Hassan's safe, not the specifics, for Hassan wanted him to hold the papers until he could retrieve them. Schmidt wanting to sell them sounded very plausible. Schneider was ready to sign off on the authenticity of what was before them.

Schneider continued. "Probably the best plan is to set up an appointment with Nasser. I would telex him saying there have been some new developments and we'd like to see him as soon as possible. In the meantime, let's have a discussion with the council and see if we could possibly develop the rockets here. Hassan was able to do so. Do any of our members have the skill and ability to develop the components? It's worth going over it again. I don't trust Nasser. He has his own agenda which, in many ways, fits with ours…the destruction of Israel."

- A Cause For All -

Schneider was adamant! "We are a strong group and many of us have excellent technical organizations. We should and must explore this option. Let's set up a meeting. I want to make sure Greta does not say anything. She may have to be eliminated."

Adler was irate. "Schneider, Greta will say nothing. You have seen her commitment by bringing the papers directly to us. I need her."

Schneider replied. "We shall see. Our safety, as well as that of our group, hinges on her not saying anything. She was visibly upset when she left…not a good sign."

When Schneider went back to his office, he sat for a moment and then dialed the phone.

"Dieter, I hope all is well. Listen, I might have some work for you in Dusseldorf. Are you able to handle a delicate situation?"

"By all means!"

"I'll send you the details: photo, address, etc. overnight. Guten Tag. It needs to happen this week. Guten Tag."

Nasser received the telex and was curious about Schneider's reason for calling. He never liked or trusted the Germans. They serve a purpose. Let him come.

Michael felt Greta needed bolstering and made a date to fly back to Dusseldorf. He would stay the night at the Steigenberger Hof. He liked it better than the Breidenbacher. He decided against the early flight and, instead, got in around one-thirty in the afternoon, getting to the hotel about an hour later. Their date was for dinner, so he decided to shop two or three stores which carried styling similar to his product lines. The afternoon went by and he headed back to the hotel to freshen up before meeting Greta.

Michael went downstairs to the business center. He had written a long telex that needed to be sent. By now, he knew the woman at the business center who greeted him. He went back to his room for a while to catch the BBC News and also try to understand a French news broadcast from Paris. They would have an early dinner, not a problem in Germany. He had also booked the small conference room in the business center to view the prototypes.

Greta came at six, slightly behind schedule because of her workload. She had not cut back at Style Haus even though it was not her future. She had handed off the tape to a Mossad agent when she arrived from Munich.

They greeted each other warmly. Greta could not hold back the tears. Michael realized he had come at the right time as she was emotionally drained from the meeting with Adler and Schneider.

"We can have dinner first and talk or we can look at the new protos and then eat. What would you like?"

"Let's eat and talk. I didn't have lunch."

The dining room was empty, and they sat at a corner table. The restaurant always served you a glass of champagne as you sat down. They clinked their glasses and smiled at each other. There was small talk and business stories. Michael recounted what he liked in the stores. A pianist started playing his set. Michael then asked her about the meeting.

"I imagine they were more than surprised and interested in your package."

"I didn't like Schneider's reaction to my being involved."

"What do you mean?"

"He was more concerned that I might say something to the police or whomever. He was interrogating me as to whether I shared any of the information with others. That bothered me. No, I should say, scared me."

"How was Adler?"

"He was apologetic for Schneider's hard line. I got the impression he did not think I told anyone else."

"Well, as far as I'm concerned, you have more than done your part, and your service has come to an end. We will make plans soon to announce your leaving Style Haus for a new venture in the United States. I am serious about this thing with Schneider. He scares me also. He is a hard-core Nazi and capable of doing bad things."

"Michael, I can handle it as long as it's necessary."

They finished dinner, lingering over coffee. They walked over to the business center where Michael showed her the new prototypes he had worked on in Paris.

- A Cause For All -

"Michael, they are really great. They have a very fresh look. I'm really pleased. The color palette will be important. There's a lot of potential here!"

"Greta, give me a minute. I'm going to run up to the room. I'll be right back."

His training by the Mossad made Michael very security conscious. He wanted to take her home and reached for his gun and fitted the silencer. He put an extra clip in his pocket. Michael did not want to alarm her any more than necessary, but he was not happy with Schneider's comments. Better to be safe than sorry. He would arrange for her coverage by the Mossad tomorrow.

Greta didn't live far from the hotel. A walk through the Old Town Altstadt would be nice and her apartment was close to the Rhine. Michael didn't realize that Greta was followed when she left her office and went to the hotel. Dieter Keller had all her information from Schneider and had accepted the "sanction". He did not expect her to go to the hotel and was surprised when Michael joined her and they started walking, presumably to her apartment. At first, he didn't know how he should proceed or whether he should delay the "hit". But then, he thought if he killed them both and they were robbed, it would work. He didn't know but got the feeling that Michael was a foreigner, probably a businessman who Greta picked up at the bar or, at most, a hot date.

It was a little chilly and Michael was wearing his trench coat. He and Greta chatted as they walked over the trolley tracks and down into the Old Town. There had to be thirty beer haus and taverns, between them and her apartment, probably more. They strolled down the Andrea Strasse. There were a few very young fashion boutiques along the way and they stopped at every one. Michael's training gave him an acute awareness if he were being followed. The windows of the boutiques served the purpose of allowing surveillance on his part. He was super-sensitive since his altercation with Schmidt's team.

Michael was certain he was being followed; however, he could also tell it was not a truly professional stalker. Greta had no idea, and he didn't want to say anything until it was absolutely necessary. They continued on the Kurze Strasse and began walking through areas with fewer shops and activity. It would be more difficult to track his follower's movements. At the same time, they were getting closer to Greta's flat. They could smell the Rhine and the wind was picking up. When they reached her neighborhood, he finally felt he needed to say something so she would take on a defensive posture. He grabbed her by the arm and pushed her close.

"Greta, listen carefully. Someone is following us. I want you to do exactly what I tell you to do when I say it."

Almost unable to speak, she whispered, "I will."

"How far is it to your apartment?"

"We are two and a half blocks from my door."

"I expect him to move in closer to us as if he is out for a walk or lives very close to you. When I say 'now', you will drop to the ground immediately. I have a weapon and am trained to use it. In fact, I am a very good shot. We are in good shape. I would say that he does not believe I am armed, which is to our advantage. So, let's stay cool and, hopefully, I am wrong, and my instincts need rewiring."

Dieter Keller had done other work for the Aryan National Party. He was an ex-Nazi and a Waffen SS. He had been on the Russian Front, where he was wounded and carried the scars from shrapnel injuries. After the war, he spent his years working for the local Munich government. He was just over forty years old and about five foot eleven with a normal-sized frame. As far as he was concerned, this would not be a problem as he enjoyed murder. He would kill them within the next block and a half and rob them. It would create headlines in Dusseldorf, depending on who the man was. He felt his pocket for his silenced Walther pistol.

There were cars parked along the street and Michael used the mirrors to keep track of his assailant. Greta was holding his arm for dear life, afraid to say a word.

Michael felt it was time to make his move. They were nearing the apartment and it was not well lit. There was an open space on the street and a Mercedes sedan was parked just two doors down from her building. Michael suddenly pushed Greta off the sidewalk into the bushes along the sidewalk and jumped with her. Keller was caught off-guard and lost his advantage, bringing his pistol out, firing off two shots.

Michael took aim and hit him in the right thigh. It did not stop Keller from firing again, but Michael did not have to consider firing back. Dieter Keller received two bullets in his neck. Avrom, a Mossad agent who Michael knew from his work in Egypt, came running over to check the corpse. Within twenty seconds, a van pulled up and the body was gone. Michael had no idea how they got there. He later learned they had been covering Michael and Greta's every move in Dusseldorf. The van was already on its way to dispose of the body.

Michael took Greta into her apartment. "Greta, you have a passport. Get your things together. You are coming to Paris with me and then to London and the States. Don't worry about the wardrobe. We will outfit you! Your days in Germany are over for now. You're not staying here tonight. I will get you a room at the Steigenberger. It's too late for a flight to Paris. Your friends in Munich weren't taking any chances of you talking. Would you call a taxi? Avrom is downstairs making sure the killer acted alone. No one heard anything as all the guns had silencers."

Greta was speechless. She hugged him.

Michael was on the phone when they were back at the hotel. He managed to get her a room next to his and made sure she locked the door, letting no one in. Avrom rode with them back to the hotel and took up a position in front of her room until the morning, when they took the first flight out to Paris.

Chapter 28

ARON AND JOSHUA had been in London and met them in Paris. "We now have to re-think part of our plan. Their man will not call to verify Greta's death. They won't know what to think. Did he kill her in her apartment? Why is he not checking in?"

Aron took all of his identification before they disposed of his body. "It will be some time, possibly only through dental records, until they are able to identify him. Now, where are we?'

Schneider expected a call last night, no later than the morning, to verify the kill. When the call didn't come, he got in touch with Adler. "Have you heard from Greta? I imagine she is still shaken up over her brother. I'm concerned about her. I think I'll give her a call in the office. She is usually in early."

"I just called her. She is not in and I also tried her apartment. It's very strange."

"Adler, we may have a problem."

"What are you talking about?"

"It's a situation we cannot discuss over the phone. I will come over shortly."

Joshua began the discussion. "They now know, or will very shortly, that Greta was working for us. We have Keller's identification and he will not be found. They will be in a state of panic, at least initially. How do we take advantage of their confusion and fear? I think we can possibly try a long shot. What do you think of this idea?"

Adler could not believe what he was hearing. "You hired someone to kill Greta and you did this without telling me. How could you do that? Did he kill her?"

"I don't know."

"What do you mean, you don't know?"

"I haven't heard from him!"

"You're insane. What have you done!"

"I am sorry to interrupt you but there is an urgent call for Mr. Schneider."

"Mr. Schneider, I want you to listen carefully. I will not repeat the instructions. This is the Red Army Faction calling. It is not a prank. We are very serious. We represent Greta Schmidt, sister of Walter Schmidt, who is affiliated with us. There was an attempt on Greta's life last evening by a Mr. Dieter Keller, who unfortunately was killed in a shootout with our people. Just so you know this is true, within the hour you should be receiving via courier his identification papers along with a photo of his body. Greta is now safe. We have a copy of everything she handed over to you and a recording of the conversation she had with you and Herr Adler in Munich. We are demanding a payment of five hundred thousand United States dollars or its equivalent in British pounds by tomorrow evening or all this information will be forwarded to the proper authorities. This is not open to negotiation in any way. You have approximately thirty-six hours to make the payment. You will hear from us shortly. Guten Tag."

Bengy delivered the message in German. Michael was beaming. "You Jews have a strange way of making someone sweat! I want that money for Greta."

Michael went to London to see Sir Arthur. "We have some new developments that could be interesting. Your involvement with us centered around the scam to buy Style Haus. Well, what if I told you I could steal it, buy it for half price, possibly less!"

"I would say you are a mashugana. We went through the exercise with the Germans, even though it was a charade. I think this can be done. I need some time to work it out. Are you interested?"

"Possibly!"

"Are you interested in buying it with me?"

"Sounds interesting."

"Let's see what happens."

The main objective now was to create as much havoc with Nasser as possible. They had achieved somewhat of a coup by having Fatah bring the plans to Nasser, which would use his resources in a project leading nowhere.

Schneider and Adler were in shock. They underestimated Greta and were now in a situation that could not be compromised. They had to pay. There was no choice. Adler made Schneider make the five hundred thousand payment. Even so, he wanted his pound of flesh from him. They could not comprehend what had occurred. The answers weren't forthcoming, and the facts didn't add up. What had happened was an enigma. Tel Aviv believed Schneider would cancel his meeting with Nasser.

When Greta calmed down, Aron and Joshua went over all her information. She had met a large number of ex-Nazis at the gala event and also in Adler's company. Greta brought a list of the group. There were twelve names along with a brief description of what each person did. It was much more extensive than they expected. "What I had to do to get this list should never have to happen again!"

Chapter 29

Aron gave his thoughts. "Israel is enmeshed in a complicated situation. Our job right now is to find a way to help. This has come about because of aggressive intent, miscommunication, and wrong information on the part of many of the countries involved in our neighborhood. There are outside participants. I told you earlier, the Soviet Union is easily involved with our friend, Nasser. He has misled, not only Egypt, but also Syria into believing we have troops on their borders ready for an attack. We are trying to negate these misconceptions by inviting the Soviet Ambassador to the front. The escalation is serious. Israel does not want war, not at this time!"

"This Soviet manipulation has led to large Intra-Arab troop movements directed against us. So, what we thought would happen has occurred. An Arab movement, led by Nasser, as champion of Pan-Arabism is now in progress. We now have to make difficult decisions in order to placate these adversaries or plunge ourselves into a conflict. It has taken us three wars, untold deaths and suffering to keep Israel safe. We would hope there is not another conflict on the horizon, but we must realize what is on the horizon."

"Egypt has now formed a military pact with Jordan, Iraq, Algeria, Saudi Arabia, Sudan, Tunisia, Libya, and Morocco. They are all in the process of sending troops for the coming fight. We have had guarantees from the 1956 Suez War, in which we evacuated the

Sinai in return for a United Nations buffer force, as well as assurance from the western allies for free passage through the Straits of Tiran to Elat. All we are hearing as we monitor broadcasts throughout the Arab world is: 'We shall destroy Israel inhabitants and drive them into the sea!'. Not a new line, but now it seems to be bothering us on a different level. We are experiencing problems that are affecting our economy because of these events that blockade our access to the sea. If this continues, we could bleed to death from a flesh wound. What are we to do? Wait for diplomacy which, as we all know, has not been kind to Jews and Israel. The armies of one hundred million Arabs are forming to strike us. So, I will say it again. We must help now! This waiting is impossible. Everyone is being called up and mobilized. We cannot maintain this state of readiness."

Joshua countered. "Michael, you're the resident genius among us! Can we find an answer?"

Michael took the pointer from the blackboard. They talked late into the night. The blackboard was erased and redrawn every hour.

"We know what needs to be done. If we do not grasp the advantage, we will be pissing against the wind. The major plan is to use our strength. We have the best pilots in the world. No one is at this level; even the United States is not in our class. We have outfitted our fighters with the most innovative equipment. We are able to fly more than double the number of sorties."

They came up with ideas and, one after another, they were discarded.

Michael looked at Aron and Joshua. "Who knows Egypt better than me or Bengy? We need to be there to make a difference. The answer and the plan must be centered there."

Joshua got up. "Michael, are you crazy? You are not going back. Nasser will kill you. You are pushing your luck."

Michael started to use the blackboard, stopped as if the lights went out, and threw the chalk at Joshua. "I am going back as an Egyptian business person, part owner in a cement/asphalt company that has a contract to service and repair the runways of the Egyptian Air Force. Bengy will accompany me as my German partner, as well as having business dealings with Nasser. Let's get started!"

Joshua and Aron looked at each other in amazement.

Michael started to speak. "This is our advantage and we have to find a way to maximize our aircraft. The main concern is Egypt with its Air Force of over three hundred planes. Our strength has been to penetrate their organizations. We have destroyed their facilities, fooled their people and caused complete disarray. We are not going to do anything that would be meaningful while we're sitting here or even in Israel. We need to go to Egypt and find a way to help our boys destroy their Air Force. Now that we have settled that, let's come up with a strategy. Let's get out the maps and see where we begin."

Michael phoned home. Doria was full of news. Her mother was doing well. "My love, she is almost back to her old self. She is going for walks every day. We have a person assisting with the physical therapy and making sure she has help when she needs it. Isn't that wonderful?"

"I am quickly learning the business. I work mostly with Abe and their staff. They couldn't be nicer. This business is exciting and the plans for future development will be even more so. There's never a dull moment around here! How is everything going? I didn't hear from you yesterday. Is everything all right?"

"Tell Abe I will speak with him tomorrow. Take care, my love!"

"We need to be in contact with Mr. Nsar to set up a scenario that will take us to the most important Egyptian airfields. Nsar will send the information to you. Bengy, are you with me?"

"I wouldn't let you do this alone. Besides, I kind of miss Mr. Nsar."

Aron jumped in. "Let's stop for a minute and see if this can be done."

Michael had three days to become an expert on cement, asphalt and road and runway construction. He and Bengy were making their lists.

"Aron, please reach your people and have them get us a van. I would like lettering put on it. "Airport Runway Company"…we need to come up with a name. Business cards have to be made. We need uniforms of some sort. I need equipment in the van, cement, asphalt packs, tools for cement, a grooving tool. We will need passports. We'll need identity papers while we are there. Bengy will need a German passport for travel. You make the arrangements."

Michael and Bengy were checking their lists. "Bengy, your Arabic is certainly sufficient, but you do not pass as an Egyptian. I think we should keep you as a German. You should be the owner of this company in Germany and also part of a joint venture here in Egypt. Let's kick it around with Aron and Joshua."

They spent another three hours debating the plan. They decided on El Sayed Cement Company, surfacing roads and runways. The company would be based in Cairo. Bengy's cover was still being debated. The consensus was to keep him German. The key was whether or not Tel Aviv could move fast enough to put this plan into action. They were working against the clock. They needed Mr. Nsar's complete focus on lining up all the necessary pieces for the operation. Mr. Nsar was now spending most of his time doing special projects for Nasser that involved only international issues.

Michael and Bengy were ready to go. Michael had a flight from Paris to Cairo with an open ticket back to Paris. Bengy flew from Zurich to Cairo with a return through Dusseldorf. They would spend two days in Cairo organizing the van and their schedule to the airports. Michael became Mohammad El Sayed. He was the local owner of the cement company. Bengy became Kurt Hirsh, partner in the Egyptian company, which licensed the technology from his German company.

Tel Aviv had done their part as they both had at least two identities in case they were needed. Michael had said nothing to Doria or Abe. He realized what he was doing could be considered "reckless", but he felt compelled to go ahead with the plan. Israel was in trouble. What they were facing could mean being driven into the sea, the end of a way of life for over two million people. The outcome could not only affect Israel, but the world Jewry. An Israeli defeat would have consequences that could not be considered or imagined. They were willing to do whatever it took to turn the tables to their advantage. The plan was, as Michael realized, "off the wall". But, what were the alternatives? There weren't any. These were the cards they were dealt. They were drawing for an inside straight, fully aware of the odds and possible outcome. Michael called home before he left. "My love, I am off to work with the boys. I will try to reach you as soon as I can."

"I hear a different tone in your voice. Is everything all right?"

"Things are fine, but we need to clean up a few things that have been left unfinished."

"I understand. Please stay safe. I love you."

"My love, take care."

When Doria hung up the phone, there were tears streaming down her face. She knew the gravity of the situation.

Michael called Abe and talked shop for close to thirty minutes. "Oh, I am going to Israel to see the boys. I'll keep you posted."

"Michael, I know you. You are going to be involved in something you shouldn't be. It would be foolish of me to try to dissuade you. May God keep you from harm's way."

"Abe, take care of everyone while I'm gone."

They needed to meet with Mr. Nsar in a place where he wouldn't be recognized. The safest place was Nsar's apartment. Michael knew it well as he had lived in the same complex. They actually came to the meeting dressed as Arabs.

"My friend, how have you been? I didn't think I would see you here in Egypt."

"I didn't either, but here I am and, as always, we need your help. Here is a list of all the airfields we must see in three days. I cannot tell you how important this is. Israel is in peril. We need to transmit the information daily if possible. The most important point is we need to be at the three most important airfields around 8:30 am each morning. I need to see their state of readiness at that time. Here is a list of all the targets we wish to see."

Our excuse or reason to be there is that we are checking the condition of the runways. The rest of our time we'll be looking at as many additional airfields as possible. We may be able to stay an additional day. We shall see! I imagine you have a place for us to stay."

Mr. Nsar began. "We can work out your program very easily. The airfields are not that far apart, except for the base at Luxor. We shall work out the schedule and you will have it in the morning when we start. I have a safe house for you. It will be familiar to you as it's the same one you were brought to after destroying Hassan's facilities."

"I remember it clearly. It served its purpose. I hope it does the same once again."

Nsar responded. "I will not be with you tomorrow during the day, but a trusted person will take you to these places you designated. I will see you in the evening. I suggest you wear business clothes tomorrow, but I want you to change back into Arab outfits before you leave the van for the safe house. I will try to update you on any plans that will affect your mission. Do not underestimate Nasser. If he knew you were here, he would move the Great Sphinx to find you! I hope you sleep well, and may the Gods be with you tomorrow."

"Before you go, tell me…is there anything left of Hassan's factory and research center?"

"I have been back with our President to survey the ruins. Only the foundations are still intact. All the rest is gone. Between the explosion and the surge from the water towers, nothing is there."

Michael smiled. "Good night, my friend."

The van came for them at six in the morning. It would be a two-hour drive to the first stop. They were quiet as the desert loomed before them.

Chapter 30

THE LIST WAS quite long.

El Arish	Beni Sweif
Jabal Libne	Al Minya
BirGafgafa	Luxor
Bir al Thamada	Al Mansura
Abil Suweir	AB Suweir
Is Ma'Iliya	Fai'd
Kibrit	Helwan
Al Maza	

They would travel to Fai'd and start there. Entrance to the base required showing of identification and written orders. The guards at the entrance phoned headquarters for authorization. The officer in charge told them to wait and he would come down to see their papers.

Michael, in perfect Egyptian dialect, said, "Sir, we are here at the military's request to see the condition of your runways and make notes for repairs if necessary. We need approximately two to three hours to do our study, possibly less. We would appreciate your cooperation and ask that you allow one of your personnel to accompany us. I want you to meet my joint venture partner, Mr. Kurt Hirsh, who is from Germany and is here working on a number of projects with the government. Mr. Hirsh is a personal friend and has a business relationship with our President. In fact, he will see him later today. I suggest you confirm our mission so Mr. Hirsh will not be late."

The officer looked at the papers. "I do not believe that will be necessary. Let us get on with the work. I will personally accompany you. The runways seem to be in good condition."

It took them less than two hours to see the entire base. Bengy had prepared a form designating aircraft type and quantity under the headings of "types". Mr. Hirsh was making notes on what had to be done.

The officer asked. "Would you like to stay for lunch or have a coffee?"

"Thank you, but we have additional sites to see today before meeting the President. May Allah bless you."

They visited three other bases, using the same story. Mr. Nsar met them at nine pm and was given the information, which included an extensive and complete list of fighters and bombers on the ground. There were notes regarding the best times to find the aircraft on the ground when they are most vulnerable.

They went to Kibrit the next morning and used the same approach. It seemed to be working. The second in command looked at their papers and again offered to drive them around the base. They arrived slightly earlier and could not refuse breakfast with the officers. Bengy did the note-taking and Michael conversed with the officers and flight staff. They spent three hours there and were able to see the entire base. Their conversations with the pilots were a source of valuable information for them. Their day was full, seeing an additional three smaller airfields for a total of eight. They would see Mr. Nsar again this evening and pass on to him all they had learned.

There was some food in the refrigerator, but just the basics. Bengy and Michael were starving and devoured the contents. Afterwards, they sat down, trying to piece together any additional information they may have missed. Things were going along too well, and they were waiting for something to go wrong.

In the morning, their schedule was to visit Bir al Thamada, which was not conveniently located, so it would be possible to see only one additional airfield, possibly two.

Unknown to Michael and Mr. Nsar, a new Egyptian troop commander arrived near the Bir al Thamada airfield with an officer contingent and troops. He made plans to visit the airfield on the same day. When Michael and Bengy arrived at the airfield, they used the same approach to gain entrance. The duty officer met them and, just as the others did, offered to make the inspection with them. When they finished, they were brought to headquarters for coffee, which they could not refuse. Sitting there was the commander and, although very cordial, was more than curious about their work.

"Tell me, Sayed, are you working on a government contract?"

"We have contracted for repairing and grooving thirteen airfields if necessary."

"What do you mean by grooving?"

"Well, an arriving aircraft needs maximum traction, especially when the pavement is wet. There is a tendency to hydroplane. Just what it means…grooves in the runway surface. By grooving, we give the wheels the ability to grip the surface. The grooving also allows the water to run off to the sides. We perform other methods to attain a better surface. We reseal openings and potholes. Small foreign objects of any kind left on the runway could be lethal weapons, finding their way into the jet engines. It is critical to keep the runways clear of any objects. We train people to inspect them as often as twice a day, depending on the terrain and use."

The officer was impressed. "Well, you certainly know your business and we are pleased that you are working on our behalf to eliminate problems. I am not involved in this area, but I am happy to hear that we have competent people servicing this base."

Michael was cooperative. "Thank you. We have a tight schedule today. It was a pleasure meeting you."

The commander turned to the officer in charge. "Did he say they have a direct connection to our President. I hope they give you high marks for the running of this airfield."

When they got in the van, they were more than concerned. Were they believed? Would they check with Cairo? Should they go forward visiting the balance of the airfields?

Michael adjusted the car seat. "Bengy, let's say they are suspicious and call the Air Force or the government agency that oversees the airfields. At least, we have today to visit additional sites. Is it worth the risk? We have seen nine airfields. There are four additional ones we would like to see. I want to hear what you have to say."

Bengy hesitated. "I would bet you did a credible job giving your 'spiel' to the commander. He believed you, but that is not what I would take to the bank. I say we have done three out of four of the key airfields. We are close to another, so let's roll the dice. We will be there in an hour."

They arrived at BirGafgafa and used the same story. They were in and out in seventy minutes.

Chapter 31

SCHNEIDER PAID THE five hundred thousand dollars to silence the RAF. Nothing was guaranteed. He didn't know what they did with Keller's body. He was almost certain he was dead.

The tape was serious. He demanded the original. No one could guarantee he got it. He was torn on how to go forward. Was a program with Nasser still viable? Could it be Syria or even Iraq, once the rockets were ready? He had his doubts but, at the same time, he wanted to destroy Israel and was willing to do anything to make it happen. There was a tremendous amount of tension growing in the Middle East. Was it the right time to invest in a program to build the rockets?

He had the blueprints. He had researched the ability to build them in Germany. No one really wanted to spend the time, money or risk the wrath of Israel or the West German government. He had eliminated the only other option that was still out there…Nasser.

Schneider had decided that he would push his colleagues at the Aryan National Party to set up a facility to develop the V2 rockets in Germany or somewhere in Europe. Each member would pay his portion to set up the research center. They had the know-how and the finances. What was missing were the components. With the technical ability in Germany and Switzerland, there wasn't any reason why it could not be done. Security was an issue but that could be overcome. With or without Adler was his final decision. He would like the project to be done in Germany, preferably around Munich, but possibly in Essen. The Rhine Valley had all the tools and experienced labor. He was committed to Germany.

Adler was in a difficult position. He lost his lover but, more importantly, the person who ran Style Haus. His son could not handle the business. Hence, it was now not only a ship without a rudder, but also without a captain. His relationship with Schneider had become outright hostile. He was not interested in the project and wanted to separate himself from Schneider in every way. He wanted to go to the organization and have Schneider eliminated any way they wished. On top of that, he was devastated over losing Greta.

When Mr. Nsar arrived that evening, they relayed the story. Nsar had not heard, to the best of his knowledge, that anyone had checked on their credibility.

Nsar commented. "Michael, I don't really think you can say we are not under suspicion. It takes time for some of these messages to reach the correct person or agency. What frightens me is that the news would reach Nasser. If so, I would know that. As of now, I have heard nothing."

He hesitated. "I would vote for not going forward and get both of you out of the country. I will send out this batch of information tonight. I will need some time to see what Tel Aviv suggests for an escape route. We need to take our lead from them. They got both of you out last time. We have to go along with their plan. I will get back to you as soon as I hear. Hopefully, by tomorrow morning we will have some answers. One way or another, I will be here late morning."

Nasser was in Cairo, speaking at a ceremony recognizing a defense treaty between Egypt and Iraq. Nasser reiterated Egypt's claim to the Straits of Tiran. He rejected all claims that the Straits were international and stated he would use force against any ship that challenged the blockade.

The commander, whom Michael had encountered at the airfield, met with his general the next morning to discuss supplies and personnel. He went over his whole program and was in a hurry as he had plans to go on vacation. "Sir, everything is in order. I don't believe there are any outstanding issues. Oh, by the way, yesterday I saw that all was well at Bir al Thamada airfield. The base was in fine shape. In fact, I met with officials from the company that checks the runways for all sorts of problems."

The general was inquisitive. "I've never heard of a company doing that type of work. Do you know their name?"

"No, I don't. They were very professional, and they had a German with them who was a friend or business partner of our President."

The general smiled. "I do not want to question anyone who has any kind of relationship with our President."

The commander nodded. "Well, I am headed for vacation!"

"I shall return to Cairo as there's a function I want to attend, but I will be back here early afternoon. I am meeting the Field Marshal who will be landing here with his staff. There will be one of the government officials and a military Iraqi delegation with him and we will inspect our troops at the front. The Commander of Sinai was not at his post, nor was his staff during the review.

Chapter 32

WAR WAS IMMINENT but the Egyptian officer core went about their daily business with little concern for the events that were unfolding. The United Nations commander was convinced that war would break out within days and he left Egypt for Gaza. He transmitted his opinion to the U.N. headquarters.

King Hussein of Jordan felt the war was days away. He predicted the Israelis would use surprise air strikes against Egyptian bases.

The Israeli ambassador to Russia was called to discuss the situation. The Russians have been the culprit, whispering in all the Arab ears that this was the best time to attack Israel.

The Israeli Defense Force was on full alert. Yitzhak Rabin, along with the military, had gone over four operational plans with repeated revisions in regard to the Sinai and Egypt. The decision was made to go all out on the southern front. Jerusalem would be fortified, but not with tanks. There would be no action against Jordan unless there was an attack. The same decision was made regarding Syria.

The plan to destroy the Egyptian Air Force was the primary focus. The premise was to annihilate the Egyptian Air Force before a ground war started. The information Michael and Bengy were compiling became invaluable.

Israel was proposing to launch its entire army and reserves, its entire arsenal, all its tanks, and two hundred planes. The opinion of the parties was that if there was a swift victory, the international communities would not be heard from. It would be a totally different story if it lingered or was a loss. The stage was set.

Mr. Nsar arrived around noon. The material that Michael and Bengy produced was now in Tel Aviv. The directions were to discontinue the operation and wait for instructions for departing. Security throughout Egypt was on high alert because of the war footing. It seemed that no one connected the dots regarding the visits to the airfields and the Israeli intelligence operation. At least that was the belief of Mr. Nsar.

Nasser was pre-occupied with the political situation both at home and internationally. The emphasis was how to play his cards versus the West and Israel.

Michael was questioning Tel Aviv's plan. They had their papers and flights out of Egypt. He felt waiting gave them a chance of being discovered. What Mr. Nsar and Michael didn't know was that Nasser's Director of Operations received a report every three days from the airfield commanders of the conditions of readiness. In these reports, three or four of the commanders mentioned the meetings with the company that repaired the runways. It took him two days to research the situation before deciding something was not right. He was concerned about approaching Nasser as he had spoken with some of the commanders. They all reiterated the story that a German was there who seemed to be a business partner and a friend of the President. The Director was now afraid to approach the President with the information for he did not want to be involved with any of the President's private business projects, which were many. Nothing was said at that time.

Chapter 33

ON JUNE 22ND, Nasser and his Chief of Intelligence laid out their plans. They showed that Israel had completed its mobilization. Moshe Dayan was appointed Defense Minister, coupled with Israeli reconnaissance over the Sinai.

Nasser would not allow Egypt to cast the first blow. He did not want to alienate world opinion or his new relationship with France. Nasser really didn't want to fight Israel. There was a diplomatic solution and it would be an advantage for Egypt. He believed he had won a bloodless war and diplomatic confrontations. Nasser felt he had won the battle of the Gulf of Aqaba, the Straits of Tiran, and the withdrawal of the UN forces from the Sinai. They were all victories for President Nasser. With all its war rhetoric, Egypt was ill-prepared for a ground offensive. There was blunder after blunder in the readiness and movement of Egyptian troops.

The world opinion was leaning toward a solution that resembled Neville Chamberlain's speech, 'Peace in our Time'.

Nasser and his generals believed in the army's ability to defeat Israel. However, it required an all-out Arab effort. They could not do it alone. The simultaneous attacks by Syria and Jordan were pivotal to a Pan-Arab victory.

Jordan strongly insisted that its strategy was not to lose a single Palestinian village to the Israelis. It would have post-political consequences with the Palestinians. This decision resulted in a plan that divided the Jordan forces in a way that would protect a three-hundred mile border. Their plans were archaic and were blown apart when the conflict started.

Syria, on the other hand, did not cooperate. They refused to coordinate their efforts with Cairo. They were ready to move the moment Israel and Egypt declared war. They called their offensive operation "Victory", a grand offensive into Israel, which meant not defending the Golan Heights. The problem was that the army was not capable of carrying out the plan. Leadership was non-existent, equipment was faulty, and the air force was not at full force. The combined forces calculated they could destroy Israel in four days. There was the retribution factor which involved total disdain against the West. A victory would also end American and British influences in the Middle East.

There was help from the entire Arab world. They came from Morocco, Tunisia, Libya, and Saudi Arabia. The vast number of troops and equipment, fueled by the immense political pressure, seemed to be an unbeatable combination. The Arab oil producers agreed to boycott any countries that aided Israel. There appeared to be one goal and that was to wipe Israel off the face of the map.

In the United States, President Johnson was occupied in domestic politics. The most pressing issue for the United States was how Israel would react. President Johnson and his Cabinet were concerned over their standing in the Arab world and the possible intervention of the Soviets precipitating global war. United States policy was restraint as the country was in chaos after the Vietnam war and did not want to risk another foreign conflict. The answer was to lift the blockade of the Straits and allow passage.

A solution emerged calling for a declaration by maritime nations asserting the right of free passage through the Straits. The code name was "Regatta". The plan ran into problems because the European allies did not want to jeopardize their Arab oil supplies. The Israelis were realistic. Even if free passage was achieved, it would not guarantee their survival. Johnson would not guarantee Israel's security without Congressional approval, which was unlikely. The policy was that Israel should depend on the United Nations' review of the Straits issue.

The impact in Israel was dramatic. If the American president was unwilling to commit to Israel on any level, they should sharpen their swords with great haste, not that they were dull. Israel was not betting their survival on an American or UN commitment. The politics were very clear. The United States felt Israel could defeat the Egyptians and the Syrians but did not want them to make a pro-active first strike. There was debate among the Israelis centered around two camps.

1. The American plan offered no solutions to the Egyptian military threat or to Palestinian terror.
2. Going ahead with a first strike would be defying the world's only sympathetic super-power.

As far as the IDF (Israel Defense Force) was concerned, it would be impossible to maintain this level of readiness over a lengthy period. It was affecting every area of Israel's economy and everyday life.

Even though the Israel Cabinet delayed a pre-emptive strike, the army continued to build momentum by calling up reservists. Israel was not about to place its fate in the hands of another country. The IDF believed Egypt would strike first. The Americans would not intervene. Syria and Jordan would join the assault for there was confusion and a decision had to be made. The army knew that if the government listened to the Americans, the Straits would be closed, and the situation would be worse. The consensus within the military was that Egypt had to be eliminated at once if Israel was to survive. The outlook was that free passage was not the issue; it was the existence of the State of Israel. The army pressed for an order to go into battle.

The signing of an Egyptian/Jordanian treaty put to rest any hope of not acting. Moshe Dayan was sworn in as Defense Minister, which affirmed the decision to resort to military action.

There were still those who believed that the international community would let Israel fight alone and to trust the United States.

The White House delayed Israel's requests for arms. The pressure on the part of Israel on the United States was not working. The U.S. Congress was not willing to lead the country into another conflict because of Vietnam. The whole "Regatta" program fell apart, not only in the U.S. The world waffled because of oil and the Armistice Agreement by the United Nations.

Johnson sent an envoy to Nasser, who was confident that Israel had amassed thirteen brigades on the Syrian border and would attack. He feared Syria would start the conflict and draw Egypt into the war. Nasser believed that successful orchestration by the United Nations or the International Court of Justice would not work and suggested a neutral negotiator. After the Israeli Ministers' meeting in the United States with the Defense Secretary and speaking with Johnson by phone, the Mossad chief concluded that waiting to attack would gain nothing and incur IDF losses. The clock was ticking!

The IDF and the general staff did not want war but destroying Nasser was Israel's only option for survival. The concern on the part of the Cabinet was the destruction of Israeli cities. The best defense was to destroy the Egyptian Air Force on the ground. The invasion of Sinai would take place only after the air offensive was successful.

Dayan's plan was war against Egypt, not Syria or Jordan. That would come after Egypt's defeat.

There were setbacks. France cut off all arms sales to Israel, wanting to restore relations with the Arab world. Within two days after joining the government, Dayan had seized control, leading the country to war. There was conflict in the Cabinet, wanting to wait for America's supposed backing. Dayan knew the only answer was war now and destroying the Egyptian Air Force. There was a vote. Twelve were for war; two were opposed. The timing was left to Dayan and Rabin. They wanted to start before Iraqi troops entered Jordan and Egyptian commandos covered the West Bank.

The invasion was scheduled for June 5, 1967. Nasser expected an invasion by June 5th, or within seventy-two hours, but he also sensed that war might be averted and Egypt would be the main beneficiary. Financial aid would be forthcoming from the United States and the Arab world.

Egyptians were beginning to believe that a bloodless victory had been won. The truth was that Egypt was not ready for war. The army was not trained for anti-tank warfare. They had no mortars, no artillery, few tanks in decent shape, and thousands of reservists without equipment or food. The Egyptian army was run on a political basis where commands were not given on merit but personal relationships with the general staff. The generals and Nasser had no doubt that the army could defend the homeland. However, defeating Israel was dependent on an all-Arab effort.

In summary, the Arab nations were united, unlike any time in the past, since 1948. They wanted the destruction of Israel and retribution from the West for being in the Middle East. This was their opportunity.

Chapter 34

NASSER HAD ALL his commanders and staff gather for final plans on how to combat the Israelis if they attacked. They went over the procedures to keep planes in the air at all times to resist an attack.

One of the commanders spoke up. "Mr. President, the Israelis could possibly bomb the runways to prevent our aircraft from getting into the air. Can we count on the company that services the runways to leave multi trucks at our disposal so we can react quickly?"

"I don't know what you are talking about. I'm not aware of any such service. Each airfield has a supply of asphalt to repair minor holes or crevices. At least they are supposed to have such supplies. Please explain."

The commanders reiterated their stories.

Nasser immediately left the meeting after receiving information on who these people were and their descriptions. Nasser was furious. "These are Jews spying on our airfields and we have been stupid enough to have helped them. I believe the spies are the same ones who fooled Hassan and destroyed our research centers. I want their heads if they are still here! Let me contact Mr. Nsar and put out a full alert."

Early morning on June 5, 1967, as Nasser started his search, Israeli jets took off from Hatzor and Ramat David every four to five minutes, sending their groups of Mirage and Ouragan bombers.

Within a half hour, two hundred planes were in the sky headed for Egyptian targets. They flew low to avoid Egyptian radar detection, which meant they were, at times, only fifteen meters above the sea or ground. They flew west toward the Mediterranean before turning left and heading toward Egypt. Others flew down the Red Sea toward targets in the interior of Egypt. Most of them were headed toward the airfields that Michael and Bengy had "visited" and acquired information. Radio silence was strictly enforced. Their only communication was through hand signals. They reached the Egyptian coast without being spotted. In the event of a mechanical problem, there would be no calls for assistance. They would have to crash into the sea.

The Israeli pilots were world class, much better-trained than the Egyptians. They had practiced "Focus" which was the name given to the operation in a secret airfield which had mock-ups of the Egyptian airfields. Michael and Bengy's updated information gave them the advantage.

The Egyptians did little to shield their planes. They were concentrated by type. MiG's, Mikoyan, and Sukhoi SU-7 combat aircraft, Tupolev bombers each in its own base, all supplied by Russia. This allowed the Israelis to prioritize the targets. All their aircraft was exposed. The fighter jets were parked on open-air aprons, completely unprotected. At that time of the day, almost all of the Egyptian Air Force was on the ground. Michael and Bengy's information confirmed that the best time to strike was around 8:15 to 8:30 in the morning, when they returned from their dawn missions and were about to have breakfast. The premise was that Israel would strike at dawn.

The Jordanians actually picked up the Israeli jets on radar with their sophisticated system. There were a large number heading out to sea. They relayed the information to Amman who, in turn, sent it to the Defense Minister in Cairo where it was never deciphered. The Egyptians had changed their codes the previous day and had not notified the Jordanians.

The Israelis had changed their frequencies, which confused the Jordanians into thinking that the blips could be coming from American or British carriers at sea. The Egyptians were only con-

- A Cause For All -

cerned with internal Army communications and did not relay the information even when it was confirmed.

The strategy requiring dozens of squadrons rendezvousing over many targets between twenty to twenty-five minutes flying time away was almost impossible to achieve in every way. All but twelve of the Israeli jets were used in the attacks. Israel was left defenseless from the air.

Now, the commanders, along with Rabin and Dayan, waited at Israeli Air Force headquarters for the results. Israel had refined their flying tactics by reducing the turn-around time for refueling and re-arming the jets to less than eight minutes. By comparison, Egyptian time was eight hours! The Israeli command waited for the initial reports.

The lead formations passed over the seas using electronic jamming equipment, eluding detection by Soviet vessels. The first targets were Fai's and Kibrit. Michael and Bengy were there less than five days ago!

Egyptian Intelligence had concluded that Israeli jets were out of range and the planes were sitting in rows or in semi-circular arrangements. The jets went up to nine thousand feet, exposing themselves to Egyptian radar and then diving. They attacked in pairs, each making three to four passes with the first group destroying the runways by bombing and the rest by strafing.

The priority was to destroy the runways, eliminate the bombers that threatened Israeli cities and then the MiGs. The missile, radar and support facilities were next in line. Each sortie was to take seven to ten minutes.

There was a twenty-minute return flight and an eight-minute refueling and re-armament time. The pilots were ready to return after a ten-minute rest. The Egyptians were under constant attack.

The bombs that were dropped were Durendals, a top-secret device they had developed with the French. Once released, the bomb was driven into the pavement by booster rockets, creating craters five meters wide and almost two meters deep. The runways were out of commission and totally destroyed, making repairs impossible. The

Egyptian planes were trapped and sitting ducks for the cannons and heat-seeking missiles that came from the Mysteres.

At Ben Sweif and Luxor, the sixteen Russian Tupolev bombers were blown to bits. In the Sinai, Mirages and Mystere strafed the parked MiG's. Only at El Arish was the runway spared to accommodate Israeli transports.

By the end of the first wave, an average of twenty-five sorties had been carried out against Cairo West, Fa'Id, and Abul Suweir bases. The main communication cable, linking Egyptian forces in Sinai with headquarters, had been severed. The damage to the Air Force, in slightly more than half an hour, was unbelievable. The Egyptians had lost two hundred four planes, half of their Air Force.

Israel lost three aircraft in the first wave. In one hundred minutes and one hundred sixty-four sorties, they destroyed an additional one hundred seven planes, while suffering an additional loss of nine aircraft.

The final results were as follows:

- Out of the four hundred twenty combat aircraft, two hundred eighty-six were destroyed.
- A third of their pilots were killed.
- Thirteen bases were rendered out of commission.
- Twenty-three radar stations and anti-aircraft sites were also out of commission.

The Egyptian Air Force was demolished. Egyptian military headquarters called Damascus and Baghdad to go into action. The plan was named "Operation Rashid", bombing Israeli airfields at once. The Iraqis claimed technical delays. The Syrians claimed their planes were involved in training missions. No one, outside of Egyptian headquarters, knew the results of the morning raids.

There were thousands in the streets chanting, "Down with Israel". The only source of information was the government's communique. It read: *"Israel began its air attack at nine a.m. Our planes scrambled and held off the attack."*

- A Cause For All -

Nasser was not at headquarters when the news of the Israeli air attacks arrived. No one told him the truth. He remained in the dark, as no one in the Army dared to enlighten him. They all went along with the version broadcasted on Cairo radio…*"that our planes and missiles are at this moment shelling Israel."*

Nasser never got the truth until around four in the afternoon when the Defense Minister relayed it to him. The Supreme Headquarters was in total disarray. The pretense was that the United States planes, not Israel's, attacked Egypt. Nasser and his ministers agreed to maintain the fictional story of Anglo-American involvement in the war. They wanted to minimize Egypt's dishonor and have the Soviets intervene. Nasser called Iraq and Kuwait to suspend oil shipments to the United States and Great Britain. Dayan insisted on maintaining absolute press silence about the results. He wanted to delay, for as long as possible, the international pressure for a cease-fire and the danger of Soviet involvement.

Chapter 35

MICHAEL AND BENGY heard all the cheering and singing and were concerned as to what was going on. They didn't know what to expect. Only did they learn of the events when Mr. Nsar appeared. He filled them in quickly about the state of affairs and the incredible results of the air raids. He also gave them the news that Nasser finally learned of their presence. Mr. Nsar was concerned but, as they all knew, Michael and Bengy were not his priority at this time. The President was pre-occupied with more important business than the spies.

Michael was ecstatic. "We really did the job. All our efforts really helped. We dealt them a death blow. All we have to do is get home. It should be a walk in the park…maybe a run!" They both laughed.

Doria had not heard from Michael in a week. She tried to stay calm and optimistic. She had an idea he was involved with the impeding war with Egypt. She wanted to call Aron and Joshua as she believed they were the only ones who knew where Michael was. When the phone rang and she heard Aron's voice, she started to cry.

"Doria, he is fine. We are calling to tell you that we will bring him home, just like we brought all of you back. Michael has done the State of Israel so much; we can never repay him. He is with Bengy, and we are working on making this happen. Please bear with us. There are complications because war has broken out. The usual avenues are closed, but, as you know, we will find a way. I will continue to keep you informed on a regular basis. We're doing everything possible. I would appreciate this conversation between us to be private. I realize Abe and Sarah are as concerned as you. You can share what I just told you with them, no one else. Take care, Shalom!"

Aron and Joshua were involved in every phase of Israeli intelligence and, as much as they wanted to spend all their time working on the boys' escape, they were involved in winning a war.

Joshua began. "How did Doria take the news?"

"As good as one could expect. She is aware of the difficult circumstances and it will take time. What are our options?"

"There aren't any international flights leaving Egypt. The sea is not an option. We will have to bring them out over land. They will probably have to walk out."

"Well, let's get something moving."

Aron and Joshua were over-exhausted. They had been up twenty-four hours addressing, not only Michael and Bengy's plan, but all their other duties. Despite this, they did come up with a strategy. The objective was to get them to El Arish. The IDF didn't bomb the runway there because they expected to take over the base to fly in troops and supplies. El Arish was roughly four hundred kilometers from Cairo. Could we get them there was the question. The distance was not the real issue. The condition of the roads and the level of security that was now in place because of the war were the unknown factors.

It could be done in stages, bringing them to Ismailia, possibly to Alexandria and then on to El Arish.

There was a war zone all along the way. The plan would need fine-tuning and a bit of luck for them to reach their destination. The key was getting them to Ismailia. The Israeli IDF had split off into two groups from El Arish, with one heading for Bir Hama and on to Bir Gafgafa, the air base which was destroyed, and one to Ismailia. Somewhere along the way they felt they would meet an Israeli armored contingent, hopefully, before they turned south to Suez.

Ismailia was situated on the West Bank of the Suez Canal and was the home of the Canal Authority. The Muslim brotherhood considered and were allies to Nasser. There was an option of going through Alexandria, but it would be much longer and possibly more complicated.

The plan would mean traveling by car or truck through territory that was repeatedly being attacked by the Israeli Air Force and completely caught up in the horrors of war.

Aron and Joshua had some ideas for their journey. They would need disguises and papers. The channels they would normally use were now closed. They had to depend on Mr. Nsar to acquire the necessary pieces. On the one hand, putting the plan together was totally different for they were on a war footing. But, there was also a plus side. Mr. Nsar would have to acquire two Egyptian office uniforms and papers so they could move through the lines without complications. They would need a military vehicle with a driver also in uniform. He would be the same driver who had helped them avoid Hassan. Getting him here from Alexandria could be an issue. All the chaos taking place now would make it more feasible for Mr. Nsar to get what was needed for the escape. Within a day everything was in order. Michael and Bengy spent a good portion of the day studying the route with maps brought by Mr. Nsar. They felt it would be best to travel by night, at least as far as Ismailia. They wanted to avoid Israel aircraft and the crowded roadways. Mr. Nsar gave them a considerable amount of Egyptian currency in case they needed it for bribes.

Chapter 36

GRETA WANTED TO go back to Dusseldorf to get her personal belongings. She needed to go to the bank and look through her safe deposit box. She was in Paris and decided she could do it in one day.

Aron and Joshua had their hands full and had put her situation on hold. She was now, more or less, under Michael's care. She was spending time in Michael's prototype stores, actually spelling him. She had no idea he was in harm's way and was somewhat miffed because she hadn't heard from him in over a week.

There were papers in the office safe that she also needed but was hesitant to go there. It would be better to leave that for another time. No one had the combination other than her. Paris to Dusseldorf was only a seventy-minute flight and was always filled with business people making day commuter trips with a return late afternoon or evening. Actually, Greta knew a few of the people on the flight who were returning from Paris business. She wanted to get there when the bank was open. She needed some time to go over all the papers in her safe deposit box. There also was her apartment which needed to be sold. She would arrange to meet a real estate person while she was there. She was leaving Germany and there were several issues that had to be put to bed.

Greta was finishing up at the bank when she heard a commotion and what sounded like gunshots. She went upstairs to find masked women and men holding the bank staff hostage while they were cleaning out the tellers' cages.

"You! pointing to Greta, "Down on the floor or you're dead!"

Everyone was quiet except you could hear some sobbing. Greta noticed someone had been shot, a guard lay there in a pool of blood. Greta thought she was hearing things.

"Well, well, if it isn't my old schoolgirl friend, Greta Schmidt Hirsh!"

Greta looked up in astonishment. It was Elsa Goering, the RAF leader. She couldn't believe it.

All Greta could say was, "Why are you doing this?"

"My dear, we need money for our work and where is the best place to get a loan than at a bank, especially a loan you don't have to repay? We are sorry everyone was not in tune with us but that's what happens when there are obstacles. Let's take her with us. She will bring a nice ransom."

"Please, Elsa, leave me alone!"

"Too late, my dear, you are worth at least a tidy sum, maybe more."

Chapter 37

Mr. Nsar had done his part. Somehow or another, he had arranged the necessary items to allow them to start their journey. The most difficult part was bringing the driver from Alexandria to Cairo. How they managed to abscond an Army vehicle was quite a feat.

Michael thought they could make El Arish in a day and a half. It was only four hundred kilometers, but that was under ordinary conditions. The condition of the roads was questionable. Did the Israeli Air Force destroy the highway to El Arish? What are the security issues? All these questions loomed in his head as they planned for their trip.

Again, they said their goodbyes to Mr. Nsar. Michael embraced him. "My friend, I can never repay you for all you have done for us and Israel. I hope, when this is over, we will see you under more favorable conditions. May Allah keep you safe."

"My friend, I am a Jew. I have been hiding my faith since boyhood. I have risen to this position. When this is over, I will go to Israel. Shalom!"

Cairo had not felt the results of the second day of the war. The news was that the Egyptian Army and Air Force had engaged the enemy and were victorious. They were now counter-attacking Israel. Cairo was no different than before the outbreak of the conflict.

Aron and Joshua finally reached the IDF commander who was leading the attack toward Ismailia. They explained the situation and asked him to be on the lookout for them. They were anticipating heavy resistance in that area because the Egyptian air bases were generally surrounded with large contingents of troops. He would do everything possible to find them.

The military vehicle was not in the best condition and had a maximum speed of fifty miles per hour. The roads getting out of Cairo were always jammed. This night they were almost impossible with people rejoicing in the streets from the false news reports relating Egyptian victories over the Jews. Cairo seldom slept; but this night there were throngs of people in the streets, not knowing the real situation.

Mr. Nsar did not know anything about the ground war. The only information he got from Tel Aviv was the Air Force had done their job, thanks partly to Michael and Bengy.

Slowly they made their way out of the city, heading northeast. Michael got to know this section of the city when he was here a year ago. He had made it his business to study the city in case he needed an escape route. That knowledge was now invaluable. He gave the driver instructions to avoid the crowds and escape the gridlock. It brought him through his old neighborhood and he savored the memories of meeting Doria there.

The military vehicle was pretty much a version of a Russian style Jeep. Most of the Army's equipment came from the Soviets and was either sub-standard or in the service area constantly. Bengy was hoping they would not have car trouble. A breakdown would cause serious problems in more ways than one. Although they had papers, they didn't want to have to use them, except at checkpoints. Mr. Nsar had found uniforms that fit them fairly well. The Egyptian Army used a British style uniform. They were wearing a khaki, somewhat camouflage-type garment with berets. Each beret insignia was different, depending on which branch of the service you were in. They were supposed to be regular Army. What they wanted to avoid at all costs was meeting units of the Republican Guard. It was an elite group whose duties were to defend the President. In many instances, they reported directly to Nasser. Their military duties were centered on being the exclusive force protecting Nasser. They were called the "Red Division" and their insignia resembled those of the Third Reich. They were the only significant military group allowed in central Cairo. The only others were those working in the intelligence areas.

Bengy was somewhat relieved. "I guess we really didn't need the driver. You know the city far better than he does."

"We need him to play this charade. He does not speak English and, as you remember, it's the same guy who schlepped us back and forth from Cairo to Alexandria."

Going through the labyrinth of streets, they finally made it to the outskirts, but on the wrong side of the city. It would take them additional time to get back on track, but they were out of the mess. The night was warmer than usual as the lights of Cairo faded away.

Michael was in a good mood. "We should start to make better time. I didn't realize it's taken us two and a half hours to get out of Cairo. The strange part of this is no one would think we are at war. The noises we heard in the city could have been fireworks, more so than idiots shooting off their guns! Somehow or another, the government has not told their people about the air strikes. The news is only that we have been repulsed and the Egyptian Air Force is attacking."

It was just the opposite. No Israeli city had been hit. They were all on full alert, but not one bomber had crossed into Israeli air space. Michael and Bengy knew the first sorties were successful. But, they had no idea how the whole air operation had fared. During the day or without the threat of war, the road to Ismailia was not great. Driving at night in a beat-up vehicle was far from the ideal way to travel.

Nasser was at his villa outside the city. He had the ability to communicate with all his staff, services, and the Republican Guard. He finally heard the truth the day before and was infuriated. He wanted to seize control of the army as he "beat up the Defense Minister". He spoke to his Council.

"How in Allah's name did we get ourselves in such a situation, knowing full well the power of the Israelis? We believed our own press we created and now we are paying for it in spades. God in

Heaven, how could we have been so naïve? We are being outplayed in all of these situations. We have to stop the bleeding and get on with defeating these Jews!"

"Tell me, have you found out anything more about the spies who 'visited' our air bases? It is far from top priority, but they made us look like schoolboys. There is a possibility they are the same people who helped destroy our munitions and research center. They still might be in Egypt."

Nasser received a call from the General headquarters and decided, even though it was late, to go into central Cairo. He couldn't sleep and was pacing the floor. His entourage consisted of two military vehicles with two motorcycle guards whose job it was to stop the traffic up ahead and allow the President to go through any traffic jam or accident.

Michael and Bengy had run into trouble. The tires on the car were almost bald. They had struck an object on the road and were now trying to fix the flat. Luckily enough, there was a spare, not in very good shape, but it would do. They pulled off to the side of the narrow highway to fix it.

Nasser's group was fifteen kilometers down the road, heading toward Michael, as they sped to the city. The two motorcycles were approximately five kilometers ahead of the three-car caravan to clear the way.

All of a sudden, Michael saw the two motorcycles approaching. It was too late to do anything. He was unsure what they wanted.

"What are you doing out here?"

"We are on our way to Ismailia and are having car trouble."

"Your papers…and where is your driver?"

Michael and Bengy produced their documents and they were scrutinized carefully as he held the flashlight. He put the light on for them and then on their photos.

"Get on with fixing the flat and stay off the road. Our President is on his way here now."

Nasser felt the car slowing down, indicating there was something going on up ahead. "Slow down, I want to see what is happening."

Just then, Nasser's car went by with the headlights illuminating the scene. It seemed like an eternity as Michael thought he saw Nasser staring directly at him.

Nasser remarked as they went by. "Someone was on the road. It looked like military people I thought I knew. We should have stopped to see if we could help."

His driver remarked. "Our escorts gave them assistance. They were well taken care of."

Michael could not believe what just happened! Bengy was in a state of shock. They looked at one another in disbelief, realizing where they were and what they were living through.

The ground war was going well. Egyptian troops, without air cover, were in total retreat. The only serious resistance was in Jordan where King Hussein was fighting on valiantly without Egypt. He received a cable from Egypt's High Command that the United States and Britain were aiding Israel. It gave him an excuse to accept a cease-fire. All of Jerusalem was now in the hands of the Israelis.

Chapter 38

MICHAEL AND BENGY finally had the tire fixed and were still in shock at being that close to getting killed. Michael knew if they were captured by Nasser, it meant certain death. They slowly made their way to Ismailia and found the safe house that Mr. Nsar had arranged. There was no one there and the key was exactly where he was told. They did not put on all the lights, just enough to make out the things they needed. Everything had been arranged and they were exhausted. It was 4:30 in the morning when they finally slept.

Michael dreamed he was being chased by Nasser. He ran as fast as he could, but Nasser was gaining on him. As he started to awaken, Doria was there, telling him to run faster. Kicking the covers off, he woke up in a cold sweat, filled with panic. He had to pinch himself to realize he was dreaming and finally fell back to sleep.

The city was quiet, just the normal sounds of the morning movements by the business people. It seemed impossible as the war was raging miles away. They were close to the city center. Mr. Nsar had not only found the right house, but there was a garage that kept the car from view. Bengy took out the maps to plot the next move. They were not even halfway into the trip and were certain they would run into Egyptian Army personnel.

The next segment of their trip was critical. The war was raging, and they didn't have the slightest idea of who was where and doing what. They presumed because Israel was winning the air war that Egyptian ground troops were in trouble. Without air support, they would be strafed and susceptible to heavy casualties. This was good and bad news. It meant more troop movements were heading toward them. Questions could be asked. The plan was to travel again at night. Michael re-thought the plan.

"Bengy, maybe we are better off during the day. We could be mistaken by either side as the enemy. The dark can cause 'shoot first and then ask questions'. I am looking to see what we can do during the day. I realize we could run into our aircraft, but there are pros and cons either way. Let me hear your side."

Bengy was still in favor of moving at night or sundown. He worried about being hit by friendly fire. They decided to soil their uniforms to make it look like they were under fire. Bengy put a bandage on his neck. Michael asked the driver his opinion. He agreed with Bengy that they should travel at night. Both Bengy and Michael had Soviet-made semi-automatic weapons. They checked them again as they had a history of jamming.

The road seemed much darker than usual. Off in the distance they could see flashes of light. You could not hear the noise, but visually the attacks lit up the night sky. They were headed in that direction!

Chapter 39

GRETA WAS RUSHED out of the bank and into one of the waiting cars. They pushed her down on the floor and threatened to shoot her if she lifted her head. The ride to their destination seemed like an eternity. She thought they might be heading toward Cologne as she heard the train and sounds which were familiar to her. All she could think of was how did she ever get herself into this mess! Before leaving the car, they put a hood over her head and literally dragged her into the building. She was now a hostage and up for ransom!

Elsa spoke to her. "So, my friend, you are now a lady of notoriety. Your photo will be in the papers…maybe worldwide…and we will see how much people value your life. It will be interesting. You will be treated with respect as long as you are cooperative and do not try to escape."

Unknown to Michael and Bengy, Nasser and his field commander had lost control which translated into anarchy in the field. The Air Force was gone, Gaza and the Northern Sinai were in Israeli hands. The Egyptian Army was in full retreat. There was total disarray.

The Israeli plans had to be totally reworked. No one believed they could achieve their objective in less than two days. The Egyptian collapse was beyond anyone's expectation and so swift. Israeli strategy was to prevent the Egyptians from establishing their second defensive line and mounting a possible counter-attack on El Arish. The Israeli commanders pushed to seize Bir al Thamada, Bir Gafgafa and Bir Hasana. They were headed toward the Canal and Ismailia.

With the lack of military victories, the Egyptian emphasis was on political propaganda. They charged the United States and Britain with intervening in the conflict on behalf of Israel. They tried to gain Soviet support and broadcasted that British bombers from Cyprus were supplying the Israelis.

Mobs throughout the Arab world attacked the British and American Embassies.

The battle for Jerusalem was entirely different. The Jordanians fought the Israelis for every inch of the Old City. The West Bank would eventually fall to the Israelis, creating all sorts of future political issues.

The German newspapers were filled with accounts of the bank robbery and the taking of a hostage. Within hours, the Red Army Front under Elsa Goering, had posted their demands for ransoming Greta. Adler thought this actually might be to his advantage. First of all, he was laughing at Schneider, for Greta had fooled them both. She had not been a part of the RAF, but he thought she had pulled off her plan by herself. He had no idea that she was working with Michael and Israel. If he paid her ransom, she would be in his debt forever. How could he make this happen was the real question?

The driver pulled the car out of the garage just before midnight and the boys jumped in. The city was not quiet. People were in the streets milling around. You could see the flashes illuminating the night. There was lots of activity. People were leaving the city, heading west, not in Michael's direction. There were military around, and Michael wanted to get out of the traffic and head east. They were not challenged as they rode through what looked like some sort of checkpoint, as that was for vehicles moving in the opposite direction, west, and away from the war.

The highway was normally two lanes, one going east and one going west. It was now a two-lane highway going west. The road was filled with all sorts of military trucks and individual cars moving away from the conflict. Their driver had to weave his way through as if he was going the wrong way on a one-way street. They pulled off the road for a moment to assess the situation.

Bengy was nervous. "Believe it or not, we could get killed in a traffic accident, but we really don't have a choice. It's our only chance to reach our lines."

Aron and Joshua were highly involved in working the intelligence in other areas, mainly Jordan and Syria. They did all they could for now to communicate with the commanders fighting in the Sinai, making them aware of the Israeli agents. They both were cautiously optimistic, hearing from Mr. Nsar that Michael and Bengy had successfully left Cairo and were on their way to Ismailia. A sense of relief washed over them when they learned that Michael and Bengy had escaped Nasser. Little did they know how close to capture they came! They were unaware of Greta's ransom, not that they could do much about it right now.

The political infighting acting out at the United Nations was intense, with each of the countries' national interests key. The United States and USSR reached an agreement for a cease-fire. The Jordanians and the Israelis accepted the resolution. The Israelis were counting on Egypt's rejection, which did not occur. Hussein decided to fight on in the hopes of saving the West Bank. The Israelis had a mission to take control of all of Jerusalem before the United Nations Security Council voted for a cease-fire. The Israeli commander sent the famous message, "The Temple Mount is ours!" The western wall was now part of Israel, the holiest shrine.

Israel ordered the launching of Operation Lights, the taking of Sharm el Sheikh. Reconnaissance showed that the area was almost deserted. The Egyptian garrison there received only radio news of the conflict and the reports of what was happening were completely false. Most of the Egyptian forces had fled. Israeli paratroopers wiped out the remaining Egyptian force and the Straits of Tiran were now open to all ships. The Red Sea was now an option for Israeli shipping and Dayan declared the Suez Canal out of bounds.

The three Israeli forces in the Sinai were on the move. One of the main objectives was to cut off the Egyptians' primary escape route via the Friedan Bridge over the Suez Canal. The others were swinging through Bir Hasana and Bir Thamada, the third cutting off the passes to crossing the canal. No matter what route Michael and Bengy took, they were destined to run into Israeli units.

The Syrians were shelling the Galilee Ladinos and the Kitbutzim from their Golan Heights positions. They had no intention of invading Israel. Israeli public opinion strongly supported a Golan offensive. The lead article in the daily Haaretz newspaper read: "The time has come to settle accounts with those who started it all."

On the eve of June 5th, the IAF attacked Syrian airfields, destroying two-thirds of their aircraft. Those that survived the attack retreated to distant bases, never to play a role in the conflict. Syria retaliated with more bombardment from the Golan Heights. There was a debate on whether the Golan should be attacked. The estimate for casualties could be as high as thirty thousand men! There was heated debate, and rightly so.

As the war in the Sinai and the West Bank cleared, the intelligence estimated that many of the Syrian defenses in the Golan region were collapsing. They also felt that Soviet intervention had been reduced. The price for victory would be high. Was victory needed in the Golan? In the eyes of many, it was necessary. The Golan represented a threat to the Galilee and many Israeli settlements. The decision was to go forward with the invasion.

Israel had acquired excellent intelligence regarding the Syrian battle positions. The Golan offensive lasted five days of intense and, at times, hand-to-hand fighting. The terrain and the defenses that Syria had developed over a long period created massive casualties on both sides. Israel was victorious because of the constant pressure they put on Syrian positions.

On June 10th, Syrian field commanders fled, leaving their troops leaderless and new equipment unused. By June 10th, the final offensive in the Golan was completed.

The amount of traffic moving west was a total retreat on the part of the Egyptians. Equipment of all sorts was being left everywhere. It was not an orderly retreat but a humiliating rush to escape the Israelis' onslaught. Bengy and Michael had an almost impossible time going east. No one cared who they were or where they were going. The army personnel had one goal in mind…get over the canal before their escape routes were cut off. As they got closer to the battle lines, they had to decide on how to proceed. They didn't want to be killed by friendly fire, nor by the Egyptians. They would leave the car as soon as they thought they were in range of the battle or the advancing Israeli forces. They pulled the car off the road and found a secluded spot where they changed into civilian clothes. Their chances of not being mistakenly shot were much better. The Egyptians could care less who they were or what they were wearing. The car, in their estimation, was becoming a liability so they decided to leave it and walk toward the advancing Israelis.

All three started waving their white shirts and screaming in Hebrew, "We are Israelis! We are Israelis! Shalom! Shalom!" They were surrounded by the ground troops who were riding on the tanks. Bengy and Michel told their story. There were still Uzi's pointed at them. A tank commander started to search them.

Michael spoke. "Do me a favor. Call El Arish or your intelligence command. They will know who we are." Within thirty-five minutes, their identity was confirmed, and they were put in a Jeep and sent back to El Arish.

When they arrived in El Arish, they wanted to reach Aron and Joshua. Bengy had their numbers and within three hours they were talking.

"Well, we are here in El Arish just as planned. How we made it, I will never know. We have to thank our man, Mr. Nsar. He was the hero, not us."

Michael was impatiently waiting to speak to them. "Aron, we are fine. Call Doria now. She has to be crazy worrying where I am."

"I will do it as soon as I hang up. We will get you back to Jerusalem as soon as we can. It will take a few days. Just so you know, there is a war on! Tell Bengy I will call home."

When Doria hung up the phone, the weight of the world was off her shoulders. All her prayers had been answered. Her beloved Michael was safe, and she was carrying his child. All was well in the world.

- A Cause For All -

The Six-Day War was an overwhelming victory for the Israelis, but over nine hundred were killed and forty-five hundred wounded with most of the casualties coming in the Jordanian and Syrian campaigns.

Close to fifteen thousand Egyptians were killed or wounded and over four thousand were captured. The Jordanians lost six thousand and five hundred fifty were captured. The Syrians lost two thousand and six hundred were captured.

The map of the Middle East was changed. Dramatic changes had occurred with far flung implications for everyone. Israel conquered forty-two square miles, three and a half times their original size. Their territory included the West Bank, Gaza, Sinai Peninsula and the Golan Heights. There were 1.2 million Palestinians now under their control. Damascus, Cairo, and Amman were now in range of Israeli artillery. Jerusalem was united.

There was extensive displacement of the Arab population in the captured territories, about one million in the West Bank and Gaza. In the Golan Heights, an estimated eighty thousand Syrians fled. Actually, it was closer to one hundred thirty thousand.

Israel allowed only the inhabitants of East Jerusalem and the Golan Heights full citizenship. The vast majority in both territories declined. Many from the West Bank crossed the Jordan River and made their way to Jordan and beyond. A conservative estimate would put it at about two hundred fifty thousand. There was free transportation after June 11th from East Jerusalem to the Allenby Bridge which crossed the Jordan River. At the bridge they had to sign a document stating they were leaving of their own free will. As many as seventy thousand migrated from the Gaza strip to Egypt.

The Arab's position had not changed because of the war. There could be no peace with Israel, no recognition of a Zionist State. Negotiations with Israel were not an option. Nasser somehow managed to stay in power, blaming the United States and Britain for his failures. His goal was to regain the lost territories. He needed a military option and that meant rebuilding the army. He turned to the Soviets, who balked initially but agreed to re-arm Egypt. With his replenished arsenal, Nasser was able to wage a three-year war of attrition against Israeli forces in the Sinai and to sustain his claim the June war was just the first stage in the struggle and so it went on.

Chapter 40

IT TOOK FOUR days for the boys to get to Tel Aviv. They were met by Aron and Joshua and were debriefed. Most of the information they acquired was sent to them by Mr. Nsar.

They were exhausted from the ordeal, but they were not injured. Michael wanted to go home. He had been on the phone with Doria and Abe twice a day while they were being debriefed and recuperating. He found out about Greta and was in total disbelief. Aron had the information and gave him everything they knew. Michael was at first astonished and then angry. He slammed his fist against the wall and cursed the entire course of events.

"What are we going to do about this? This woman went to the wall for us and is in this situation mainly because of what she did for us. We, yes…we, have to set this thing straight! I am calling on all of you to get her out of their clutches. I am committing myself to get this done. I need you to help."

Joshua sat Michael down. "We are not going to desert her. Fortunately, our people have been keeping track of the RAF for quite some time. We know their whereabouts and have updated profiles on the Baader Meinhof gang. Michael, we would have taken care of this sooner; but we had a war to win and, by the way, get you and Bengy home. I really don't want you involved in this plan. I want you to be on a plane to Boston."

"Aron, I am not going anywhere until Greta is safe. I put her in this situation, and I will get her out. Tell me, what have you planned?"

"We will need help to free her. They are located outside of Munich, not far from Dachau. We believe Greta is there. I will assemble a team. The house where she is being held is an estate which houses their headquarters. These are bad people and there will be gunfire. I don't believe it can be avoided. We will need four to five of us to take down the opposition. I would like to do this when their leader is not there. The way to make this happen is to create confusion so we can get close enough to eliminate any opposition. We have a plan, which we will go over with you. I have already booked our flights to Munich."

Joshua had a complete layout of their headquarters. There were three buildings on the property. "This building is where they sleep. It has a conference room for meetings. This second structure has a firing range in it as well as a repair shop. The third building is where we think they are holding Greta. It has sleeping quarters and sort of a combination game room/function room/kitchen. The major problem is getting close enough to the target area without setting off an alarm. So, here is the plan!"

Adler was desperate to get Greta back. It was over eight weeks since she was running Style Haus and there were already serious problems. Greta was in the hands of the RAF and had already been held sixteen days. Adler had started negotiating to pay the ransom.

Elsa Goering knew Adler. In fact, he was a very distant cousin. She disliked him intensely, for he was a Fascist and Elsa had Communist leanings. They were like oil and water. She knew Adler wanted Greta and raised the ransom to four hundred thousand pounds, or its equivalent in dollars.

"I raised the price on this Nazi bastard even though he's my cousin. Adler is harmless and we do not have to worry about him. In fact, he will bring the money here and we will give him his prize. How has she been? I gave orders that she should be treated well. I would not like to hear otherwise. She's been here almost three weeks. So, my long-lost cousin will come with his henchman to pick her up. What he does with her is his business."

Greta had lost weight and hope. She had no idea where Michael was or whether he cared. She had given up thinking the Israelis would help. "Where are the police, the special security forces? Who can I turn to?"

Elsa came in to see her. "Well, my dear, we have good news for you. Your ex-boss has finally decided to pay your ransom."

She started to laugh. "You should be very nice to him. He is the only one who showed any interest in you. If he didn't respond, I would have had to kill you. I don't like killing old friends. I meant to ask you what you were doing in that bank? Well, tomorrow will be here soon, and you will be free."

Greta was sobbing and relieved but hated the thought that she would owe her life to Adler. How could Michael have left her hanging out to dry? She was devastated.

Adler disliked the idea of giving the money to the Communists. The Nazis hated the Communists as much as the Jews. He put them both in the same classification. Adler called Schneider and had a long conversation. He proposed they forget their differences. They were both on the same page. Adler told him about Greta and wanted him to join him in seeking Greta's release. He actually had other reasons to bring him along. If there was a confrontation, he would kill Schneider and dump his body in the RAF estate. He could not forgive Schneider for the attempt on Greta's life. He realized Schneider could turn on him and did not want him at his back. He was in a difficult situation. Elsa was a cousin and he didn't want any further dealing with her. Nor did he want her to blackmail him in any way. All scores had to be settled with Schneider, his cousin and their group. He brought two ex-Nazis with him. He was ready.

"My fucking cousin made me pay somehow or another. I will find a way to have my day in the sun. She will regret not playing ball with the Aryan Party. Jan, Kurt, we are going to pick up Greta. Let's see who will be there. I would prefer that we kill them all!" Both of them had machine pistols under their jackets.

Chapter 41

Joshua, Aron, and Bengy met Michael in Munich. They all flew different routes through London, Paris, Zurich, transferring to their destination, Munich. Aron had arranged a safe house which they had used in the past. Two of their associates who handled German affairs were already there.

Michael was now in the city where his father, David, had been killed by the Nazis. It brought to mind the course of events that took his father from him. He thought he had laid to rest all those feelings, but they were still there, probably for the rest of his life. He played his memory tapes, recounting the story he had been told since he was a child.

They were there to free Greta. In Michael's estimation, they had a score to settle with Adler and Schneider. Tel Aviv would handle that on their own. They were responsible for crimes against humanity as well as the Jews.

Michael had not given Doria and Abe the exact date of his return, but they had been in touch on a daily basis. When he arrived in Munich, he called but did not tell them where he was. They presumed he was still in Israel.

"My love, I'm almost ready to come home. I just wanted to tell you I love you and will see you soon. Pass my best wishes along to my Mom, Abe, and Sarah."

"When can I expect you? You are not up to any more shenanigans, are you?"

"I will be home soon, possibly in the next few days."

"Michael, please. Your wife and baby-to-be need you!"

"Oh, my God, how wonderful. I love you!"

They acquired a new oil tanker truck that delivers fuel to rendezvous. They had given the project to their people in Munich, who found the right vehicle and made some adjustments. They cut out a doorway so at least four to five men could be carried in the oil compartment. It was the "Trojan Horse" scenario, Israeli style. Their plan was to be allowed to enter the estate by the guards the RAF had posted at the entrance. This would enable them to drive down to the house where Greta was located. They felt certain she was there because of the reconnaissance done by their agents before they arrived. The Israeli team thought there could be five members of the gang there, possibly a sixth. Hopefully, catching them by surprise would heighten their chances of success. Unbeknownst to Michael and company, Adler already arrived with his henchmen from the Aryan group to ransom Greta. Adler made a strategic mistake. He tried to re-negotiate the ransom price.

"My dear cousin, we made an agreement and now you want to change what we agreed on. I should kill her, and I think I should kill you."

"We will pay the ransom. Here is the four hundred thousand. Let's get this over with."

"My cousin, the price is now four hundred fifty thousand. I am pissed over you trying to chisel me."

Adler realized that he could not and did not want to negotiate any further. "Listen, we want to make a deal. I misunderstood the terms. Let's get this done!"

While the negotiation was going on, the oil truck carrying Michael and company, was authorized by the guards to go to the houses. One of the Israelis slipped out and, with gun in hand, handcuffed them to a pole. The truck pulled in front of the house as two guards came running out, one with a gun drawn, to see who had arrived. Bengy was driving and Aron was seated next to him. Michael was hunched down between them. Aron put one shot in the shoulder of one of the guards and disabled him. Bengy shot the other guard in the leg and arm before he could draw his pistol. The others came out of the truck and made their way with the threesome to where they thought Greta was being held. No one had set off an alarm. Both Bengy and Aron's shots were from their silencer pistols.

They realized other people were there as there was a Mercedes sedan sitting in front of the second building with a driver whom they soon disabled. Another member of the RAF came out of the house and they cuffed him and threw him in the back seat. Michael, Bengy, and another Israeli went around the back of the house to see if they could locate Greta. There was a back door which was easily opened. They decided to attack from two positions.

Greta was lying on the bed, half awake. Ever since she was taken hostage, she had not slept more than an hour or two at a time. She thought she was dreaming and started to talk as Michael put his hand over her mouth and carried her."

"We didn't forget you. How could we possibly forget you? We already have your ticket to the States." She started to cry.

"Now comes the hard part of getting you out of here. So, stay close to Bengy and Izzah and you will be in Paris before you know it. There seems to be more people than we thought. Tell me who they are."

Suddenly a door was opening and Bengy blocked it before it was fully opened. He reached around and delivered a devasting blow to the neck that dropped the RAF member to the floor. Everyone had drawn their weapons and were at full alert. Their luck was holding. They had not created a "shoot out". They were not naïve enough to think their luck would continue.

They were going out the way they came in. When they went into the hall, two shots just missed Michael. He swirled around and put two shots directly into the side of one member of the RAF group. Bengy started firing as another person appeared and went down quickly.

Adler and his associate, hearing the shots, drew their weapons and were ready to fire. Elsa, seeing the drawn pistols, reached under her blouse and, without hesitation, started firing at point blank range at Adler and his associate. Aron and Joshua burst into the room and emptied their clips on Elsa and two other RAF people. She died in a stream of bullets. The other two were gravely wounded.

Bengy was down. Michael ran to him. He lay there for a moment. "Thanks for reminding me to wear my vest. I will be fine in a moment."

The Israelis out-gunned them and, when it was over, six men and two women were either dead or dying. All of Michael's force were alive. Two Israelis were slightly wounded. Adler and Schneider were dead. Greta was untouched.

Michael could not believe the outcome. The four hundred fifty thousand dollars was on the floor but not for long. Bengy scooped it up.

The plan was straight-forward. Get Greta and themselves out of Germany as soon as possible. Do not get caught! The estate was secluded and more than a half mile from the highway. As far as they knew, no one really knew or heard what had transpired. Only the surrounding forest heard the sounds of the gunfight. The bodies were not their problem. The authorities would eventually be called in and come to the conclusion that a "shoot-out" had occurred between the Aryan National Party and the RAF…good riddance to both!

They could rest as tomorrow was Shabbat. Michael was amazed and overcome, looking at the carnage all around him. It was hard to believe what had just occurred. His mind was racing from one incredible ordeal to another. My God, how did this happen? Can I have my life back? Is this the end?"

He turned to Aron. "My God, I shall never pick up a weapon again!" He started to throw it away when Aron stopped him. "Wait, let me wipe it down of fingerprints. Now you can do it!"

The End

Sources

HERE IS A list of the sources plus the internet.

1. The Spies: Israel's Counter Espionage War — Yossi Melman
2. Nasser: A Political Biography — Stephen Roberts
3. Yasser Arafat: A Political Biography — Barry M. Rubin
4. A Brief History of Yasser Arafat — David Brooks—The Atlantic July–Aug issue
5. The Baader Meinhof Complex — Stefan Aust
6. Screening the Red Army Faction — Christina Gerhardt
7. Six Days of War — Michael Oren
8. The Six Day War 1967 Jordan and Syria — Simon Dunstan
9. Six Days in June — Eric Hammel

10. Six Days — Jeremy Rose

11. Gideon Spies—The Secret History of the Mossad — Gordon Thomas

12. Baghdad—City of Peace: City of Blood — Justin Marozzi

13. The Internet